"If it's okay [...] and check for foo [...]," Zach said.

Maddy smiled as she arched her neck and massaged it. "Sure," she said. "Why are you asking my permission?"

He snorted. "Are you kidding me? You told me in no uncertain terms that you were in charge here."

She eyed him with a raised brow. "You're telling me you're ready to take charge now?"

Zach felt as though her gaze were singeing his skin. He swallowed and shifted slightly, surprised that his body was straining in reaction to her teasing words. For someone who was not his type, she could take him from zero to uh-oh in no time flat. He forced himself to speak lightly, with no trace in his voice of the struggle he was waging to keep himself in check.

"Madeleine Tierney. When I'm ready to take charge, believe me, you will know it."

UNDER SUSPICION

—

MALLORY KANE

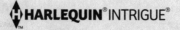

For Michael. Love you.

ISBN-13: 978-0-373-74889-1

Under Suspicion

Copyright © 2015 by Rickey R. Mallory

Recycling programs for this product may not exist in your area.

Printed in U.S.A.

Mallory Kane has two great reasons for loving to write. Her mother, a librarian, taught her to love and respect books. Her father could hold listeners spellbound for hours with his stories. His oral histories are chronicled in numerous places, including the Library of Congress Veterans' History Project. He was always her biggest fan. To learn more about Mallory, visit her online at mallorykane.com.

Books by Mallory Kane

HARLEQUIN INTRIGUE

Visit the Author Profile page at
Harlequin.com for more titles.

CAST OF CHARACTERS

Madeleine Tierney—The Homeland Security agent is on assignment to protect the wife of a slain fellow HLS agent when she meets and is instantly attracted to his oldest friend, Zach Winter. When danger strikes, she discovers that together they are unstoppable.

Zachary Winter—Zach is a newly trained undercover agent for the National Security Agency. Although he's in Bonne Chance on leave for Tristan DuChaud's funeral, when he and Maddy Tierney team up to check out odd happenings around Tristan's house, he realizes he's never felt more alive or powerful than when working beside Maddy.

Tristan DuChaud—The Homeland Security agent working undercover on a Gulf of Mexico oil rig died in an accident...or did he? His body was never recovered, leaving his pregnant wife to believe he might still be alive.

Sandy DuChaud—Tristan's pregnant wife has tried to accept that her husband is dead, so she agrees to go to Baton Rouge for her own safety. But if she finds out there was no body in the casket that was buried in Tristan's tomb, will she come back, possibly stepping right into the enemy's trap?

Boudreau—A born and bred Cajun, Boudreau lives in the swamp, and a lot of people, including Zach Winter, believe there's something wrong with his mind. But Maddy is convinced that the Cajun who was like a father to Tristan knows a lot about the smuggling operation she and Zach have helped uncover.

Murray Cho—The Vietnamese fisherman owns the old seafood warehouse where Zach suspects the smuggled weapons will be stored. When confronted, Cho claims to know nothing about smuggling or people sneaking around Tristan's house. But Zach can't afford to trust him.

Captain Poirier—The captain of the oil rig on which Tristan died is incensed that the Coast Guard or anyone else is questioning his honesty and authority, but he's the obvious choice to be the mastermind of the gun-smuggling operation being run from the rig.

Vernon Lee—The owner of a multibillion-dollar corporation with satellite businesses all over the world. He has never been fond of the spotlight and is almost a recluse. One of his companies owns the oil rig where Tristan died and where the smuggling operation is based.

Chapter One

The rain had finally stopped. Zachary Winter turned off the windshield wipers of his rental car as he passed the city limits sign for Bonne Chance, Louisiana. Now that the sun had come out, steam rose like tendrils of smoke from the blacktop road and clung to the windshield like shower spray on a mirror. He put the wipers on Intermittent. Rain in south Louisiana was seldom a relief, no matter what the season. Even in April, when most of the country was experiencing spring weather, an afternoon thunderstorm might cool the heat-soaked roads enough for steam to rise, but the tepid, humid air never seemed to change.

The last time he'd been here, in his hometown of Bonne Chance, was more than a decade ago. The name Bonne Chance was French for *Good Luck*. His mouth twisted with irony. Had his sad little hometown ever been good luck for anybody? He'd certainly never intended to come back. And the reason he was here now was not his choice.

He drove past two national chain grocery stores and a Walmart. "Well, Bonne Chance," he muttered, "I guess you've arrived if Walmart thinks you're worthy of notice."

As he turned onto Parish Road 1991, better known as Cemetery Road, a pang hit his chest, part anxiety, part grief and part dread. He'd intended to get into town in time for Tristan DuChaud's funeral. Tristan had been his best friend since before first grade.

As he rounded a curve, he spotted the dark green canopy that contrasted with the dull granite of the aboveground tombs peculiar to south Louisiana. From this distance, he couldn't read the white letters on the canopy, but he knew what they said: CARVER FUNERAL HOME, Serving Bonne Chance for Over Forty Years.

He parked on the shoulder of the road, glanced at his watch, then lowered the driver's-side window. The air that immediately swirled around his head and filled the car was suffocatingly familiar, superheated and supersaturated from the rain.

One hundred percent humidity. Now, *there* was a hard concept to explain to someone who'd never been to the Deep South. How the air could be completely saturated with water and yet no rain would fall. He usually described it as similar to breathing in a sauna. But that wasn't even close. The air down here felt heavy and thick. Within seconds, a combination of sweat and a strange, invisible mist made everything you wore and everything you touched damp. And with the sun out and drawing steam from people as well as roads and metal surfaces, it could be disturbingly hard to breathe.

Getting out of the car, Zach shrugged his shoulders, trying to peel the damp material of his white cotton shirt away from his skin, but he knew that within seconds it would be stuck again. Then he took off his sunglasses. They had fogged up immediately when the damp heat hit them. Without their protection, however, the sun's glare made it almost impossible to see. He shaded his eyes and squinted at the small group of people who were gathered around the funeral home's canopy. Most of them were dressed in black. The men had removed their jackets and hung them over the backs of the metal folding chairs set up under the canopy.

He wished he could leave his jacket in the car but that was out of the question. He'd always found it more efficient to travel armed, in his official capacity as a National Security Agency investigative agent. Today, though, a storm had hit New Orleans about a half hour before the

plane's arrival time and not even his high-secu-
rity clearance could clear the runway in time for
him to rent a car and make it to Bonne Chance
for Tristan's funeral service. It looked as though
he'd barely made it to the graveside in time.

He grabbed the jacket and put it on, then blew
on the sunglasses to dry the condensation. He
held them up to the light for inspection and put
them back on.

As he walked toward the stately aboveground
tomb that held at least three generations of the
DuChaud family, he tried to sort out the people
gathered there. Townspeople, family, friends
like himself. But his sunglasses were fogging
up again.

He approached slowly, breathing in the smell
of freshly turned earth that mixed with the fishy,
slightly moldy smell of the bayou, an unforget-
table odor he'd grown up with and hadn't missed
for one second in the thirteen years since he'd
been gone.

Zach had pushed the speed limit as much as
he could, considering what he knew about speed
traps in south Louisiana, and still he'd not only
missed Tristan's funeral, he'd almost missed the
graveside service. It was just as well, he supposed. He'd dreaded seeing his classmates, most
of whom had settled down in Bonne Chance
like Tristan, and spent their lives working on

oil rigs or fishing. He hadn't looked forward to answering their half-deriding questions about *life in the big city*.

Tristan DuChaud. His best friend, for as long as he could remember, was one of the finest people Zach had ever known. Maybe *the* finest. His gaze went to the carved stone of the tomb, its thick walls and ornate steeple soaking up all the warmth and sunlight and leaving Tristan's final resting place cold and dank.

It was strange and sad to be here, knowing his friend was gone. Especially since their last conversation had been a fight, about Sandy, of course. It had occurred two days before Zach, his older sister, Zoe, and their mom moved from Bonne Chance to Houston three days before Zach's fifteenth birthday. Sandy was mad at Tristan for some reason and she'd come to Zach's house to talk, just as she'd always done.

Tristan and Sandy had *liked* each other ever since third grade and everybody knew they'd get married one day. They were *that* couple, the one that would be together forever. But Tristan had always had a jealous streak, and that irritated Sandy to no end. Sometimes she'd egg him on by flirting with Zach, which infuriated Tristan, even though, or maybe because, he and Zach were best friends.

As Zach got closer to the grave site, the formless figures shimmering in the heat began to coalesce into recognizable people. The stocky man holding the Bible was, of course, Michael Duffy. His thick shock of light brown hair looked a little out of place above the black suit and white priest's collar he wore. Zach had heard from his mother that Duff had become a priest after the awful accident the night of Zoe's graduation, but he'd found it hard to believe that the fun-loving, hard-partying Duff was now a priest.

Duff raised his hand and the small group of people moved to sit in the folding chairs. Zach finally spotted Sandy, Tristan's wife—or widow. She looked as though she was doing okay, but for some reason, she was being led to the first chair by a woman he didn't recognize.

He studied the woman. She was about the same size as Sandy—maybe more slender. He couldn't place her. Was she a relative of Sandy's? Of Tristan's? He didn't remember ever seeing her before, and he would have remembered her. She had an intensity that he wasn't sure he'd ever noticed in a woman before.

The woman got Sandy settled then straightened and glanced around. She didn't seem to be looking for anyone in particular, but the tension that wafted from her like heat still reached out to him. He watched her, his interest piqued, not so much by her appearance, although she was attractive. He was interested in what she was doing.

Surveillance. The word popped out of his subconscious. He rolled it on his tongue. *Surveillance.* The woman was doing surveillance of the area.

As the woman checked the perimeter of the grave site, Zach noticed a subtle shift in her demeanor. She hadn't moved, but something about her had changed. When he'd first noticed her, she'd been alert, but she'd reminded him a bit of a mother hen, scurrying to keep up with Sandy, her chick. That impression had faded when she'd begun surveying the area.

Now there was nothing left of the mother hen. The woman was poised and taut in a way she hadn't been before. As he watched, she straightened, her entire focus as sharp and unwavering as an eagle that has spotted its prey.

As Zach watched her transform from protector to predator, an electric hum vibrated along his nerve endings. He felt attuned to her, as though he knew what she was thinking, what she was planning. She stepped closer to Sandy, her weight evenly balanced between her feet, her focus unwavering.

He followed her line of vision and saw two men. Like many of the others, they were dressed in slacks and a shirt with no tie, as if they'd taken off their jackets because of the heat. But these two stood at the edge of the canopy with their hands in their pockets rather than sitting and they seemed to avoid looking at anyone directly.

Zach thought there was a family resemblance between the two, although the younger one looked as though he might still be in high school. So they were probably father and son.

He glanced back at the woman. He couldn't tell if she knew them, but he could tell that she was expecting trouble.

Her intensity fed his. His scalp began to burn. His senses focused to a razor-honed sharpness as time seemed to slow down. His entire body tightened and he instinctively shifted his weight onto the balls of his feet. An almost imperceptible vibration hummed through his muscles and tendons.

At that instant, as if his energy had reached her, the woman looked directly at him. A knife edge of caution sliced into his chest. He'd never seen her before, but in that instant when her gaze met his through the shimmering heat, he had a sinking feeling that before this day was over, he was going to wish he hadn't seen her now.

Her gaze slid away from him and back to the man and boy. Again, Zach looked, too. The boy was whispering to his father. He nodded in the direction of the woman and Sandy, and the older man shook his head no. He urged the son closer to the lined-up chairs as Duff called for everyone to bow their heads for prayer.

Duff began his supplication to the Lord without bowing his own head. As he spoke, he looked Zach up and down, nodded in recognition and tilted his head disapprovingly all at the same time. Zach stood still, clasped his hands behind his back and bowed his head. But he couldn't close his eyes. He kept the two men in his peripheral vision. If they moved suddenly, he wanted to know.

Once Duff said amen and raised his head, he held out a hand to Sandy to approach the dully gleaming casket, which was sitting on a wheeled cart, waiting to be placed into the DuChaud vault. Sandy stood, and her companion started to stand beside her, but Sandy stopped her with a small gesture. Alone, she approached the casket and laid a white rose on top, bowed her head for a brief moment, then turned and started back toward her chair. Then she saw him.

Her face, which had been set determinedly, dissolved into anguish at the sight of him, and tears filled and overflowed her eyes. "Zach," she whispered. "Oh, Zach, he's gone. Our Tristan is gone."

Zach took two long strides and gathered her gently into his arms. He closed his eyes and hugged her to him as if she were his long-lost sister. She clung to him the same way, and her slender shoulders shook as she cried silently. Zach held her while Duff gestured to Tristan's mother to come forward and lay a white rose next to Sandy's. After Mrs. DuChaud sat, the priest led the pallbearers past the casket to lay red roses on top, one by one, and back to their seats.

Then the priest laid his left hand on Sandy's shoulder and held out his right toward Zach. "Zachary Winter," he said. "I thought you swore you'd never come back here."

"There's only one reason I would, Duff. I mean, Father…" Zach had no idea what to call him.

Duff smiled and said, "It's Father Michael, but Duff is fine. Nobody around here dares to call me that."

Zach nodded uncomfortably, then leaned in closer to the other man as a couple came up to offer Sandy their condolences.

"What happened?" he asked in a low tone. "How did Tristan die?"

"From what I understand, he was walking along the catwalk on the bottom level of the oil platform with one of the Vietnamese roughnecks and he fell into the water near the drill mechanism."

"Oil platform?" Zach said in surprise as a knot formed in his stomach. "He was on an oil rig? What was he doing there?"

Duff's gray brows rose. "You don't know? Have you not talked to Tristan in all these years?"

Zach shrugged, embarrassed. "Not really. We didn't talk to anybody after we moved. You know, with Zoe being involved in the accident."

Duff grimaced briefly as he nodded.

"Nothing more than an email at Christmas. A comment on Facebook. You know."

"His dad was killed on a rig about two months before Tristan's high school graduation, so he dropped out and went to work on the oil rig to help his mother."

"But he was going to LSU. He was going to be a veterinarian. How could two months have made a difference?"

Duff nodded grimly. "I talked to him, but he was determined. He saw it as a choice. Taking care of his family—he and Sandy were planning to get married right after graduation—or taking care of himself. He chose his family."

"Right." Zach's throat closed up. He felt sad and angry. Tristan had given up his education and the opportunity for a great career so he could go to work right away. The thought made Zach feel sick as he thought of all Tristan had given up. And for what? To end up dead at the bottom of the Gulf of Mexico?

"Wait a minute, Duff. Tristan had lived on boats and docks and floating logs on the Mississippi River and on the Gulf his whole life. He was the strongest swimmer I've ever seen. He couldn't have fallen overboard and drowned if he tried. What happened out there?"

"I wish I could tell you more but I can't," Duff said. "He went over with another guy, a roughneck. Maybe they were arguing or even fighting. Maybe they ran into each other in the dark."

"You know as well as I do it's never dark on an oil rig. What'd the autopsy say?"

Duff looked surprised. "The autopsy?"

Zach thought he'd hesitated for an instant. "The autopsy. Who did it?"

"I guess that would have been the ME, John Bookman. He's the medical examiner for the parish and chief of emergency medicine at the Terrebonne Parish Hospital in Houma."

"Okay. Houma is about twenty-five miles north of here, right?" Zach asked.

The priest nodded, then gestured with his head. "See Angel?"

Zach followed his gesture and saw Angel DuChaud, Tristan's ne'er-do-well cousin, talking to a small wiry man. Again, he was surprised. Three years older than he and Tristan, Angel had been the stereotypical bad boy all their lives. But he cleaned up nicely. His hair was styled and his suit fit impeccably, and hid his tattoos.

"The man he's talking to," Duff said, "is the parish medical examiner."

At that moment, Sandy turned around and took Zach's arm. He smiled at her and patted her hand.

"It's so good of you to come, Zach," she said.

"You know nothing could keep me from being here," he replied.

Duff took Sandy's hand from Zach's arm. "Sandy, walk with me over here. I want you to meet—"

Zach silently thanked Duff for distracting Sandy. He hadn't expected the parish medical examiner to be at Tristan's funeral, but he was grateful for the opportunity to ask him some questions. He walked toward Angel and, eventually, Tristan's cousin saw him.

When Angel spotted him, he waved. Zach sketched a half wave in the air and walked over to where Angel and the ME stood. Angel made casual introductions.

"You're the ME," Zach said to Dr. John Bookman. "Call me Zach. I was Tristan's best friend in school."

"I'm sorry. Terrible thing that happened to Tristan," the doctor said.

"Do you live here in Bonne Chance?"

"No," the doctor answered, eyeing Zach narrowly. "I live in Houma. Didn't Father Michael tell you that?"

Angel wandered away toward the DuChaud family crypt. Zach was glad. He didn't want him to overhear his next question. "I want to ask you about Tristan DuChaud's death."

Bookman's eyes shifted toward the casket, which was still sitting in front of the vault. But now the vault door was open. "I don't discuss my work, certainly not at a funeral."

"I understand. If I may…" Zach paused, wondering if what he was about to do was a mistake. After all, he was here not in his official capacity but just to mourn the death of his best friend and to show his respect for his widow. He decided it didn't matter whether it was a mistake. He needed to do it, for Tristan.

The question of what his boss would say flitted into his mind but he chased it out again. He'd worry about that later, if it came up.

He leaned in, close to the doctor's ear. "I'm with the National Security Agency." That was true. "We're investigating possible terrorist activity in the area." That was sort of true but not really. They *were* picking up chatter in the area around New Orleans and Galveston.

He went on. "I need to know what the cause of death was for Tristan DuChaud. Was foul play involved in his death?"

Dr. Bookman's eyes went wide, then narrowed again. He took a half step backward and studied Zach as if he were a slide under a microscope. After a moment, he asked quietly, "Did you say NSA? Shouldn't you be talking to the Coast Guard? They're in charge of the recovery."

"I need this information, Dr. Bookman."

Dr. Bookman fidgeted, obviously uncomfortable. "Do you have ID?"

Zach groaned but pulled his badge holder and ID out of his back pocket and handed it to the doctor and waited. The doctor discreetly glanced at it, looked at it again for a beat longer and then handed it back.

"You might want to meet me at the parish morgue after the service," he said quietly.

"No," Zach said. "I need to know now." He looked over at the groundskeeper, who was standing behind the cart that held Tristan's casket. "After the service could be too late."

Bookman followed his gaze. "I'm not comfortable with this. We should talk in my office."

Zach shook his head.

"Okay, but please remember that you are at the funeral of your best friend, and don't create a scene."

The medical examiner took a step away from the crowd. Zach followed him, his scalp burning at the doctor's statement. *Don't create a scene.*

"We don't have a cause of death," Bookman said.

"You what?"

"Lower your voice, Mr.—or is it Agent—Winter? You don't want to upset Sandy."

"Why don't you?" Zach asked quietly, afraid he knew the answer.

"Because we don't have a body."

Zach stared at him, then darted a glance at the casket.

"That's right. That casket contains no human remains."

"Son of a—" Zach stopped himself and rubbed his face. "You didn't recover the body?"

Bookman sighed. "I have remains."

"I don't understand," Zach persisted.

Bookman looked across the crowd at Sandy. Zach followed his gaze. "It's pretty simple. There's not enough of Tristan DuChaud to put in a casket."

"Not enough—" Zach felt queasy. He'd known that was the answer, but to hear it stated like that, in no uncertain terms, stripped him raw. "What do you mean, not enough?" he growled.

Dr. Bookman searched his face for a moment. "A rather substantial piece of calf muscle, a piece of scalp with hair intact and…that's about it. Barely enough to provide identification. I can't afford to waste any of it by burying it in the ground. Now understand, I haven't positively identified these remains with DNA. I've sent the samples off, but it generally takes weeks, if not months, to get DNA back."

The doctor might as well have sucker punched him. The idea that all that was left of Tristan was a little muscle and a bit of hair. The back of his throat burned with nausea. "What about the other man?"

Bookman nodded. "He was pretty chewed up. There were several schools of sharks in the area."

Several schools of sharks. Zach tried to erase that phrase from his mind. "But you can identify the difference between him and Tristan, right?"

"On a superficial level, yes. I can. From physical attributes mostly. The Vietnamese man, according to his employment records, was five inches shorter than DuChaud. I would expect his torso, parts of which we recovered, to be smaller than DuChaud's. I would also expect the typical Asian features, whereas DuChaud was Caucasian. I'm relatively sure that the calf muscle tissue and the scalp with light brown hair belong to DuChaud."

"What's your conclusion? Any sign of foul play?"

"I can't answer that question. Right now, what I can say with relative certainty is that I have the remains of two men, one Caucasian, one Asian. There is enough of the Asian's torso present to be certain that he perished. The meager remains we collected for DuChaud are not conclusive at all, but judging from the damage to the Vietnamese man's body, it would be difficult to imagine that DuChaud could have survived."

Zach swallowed hard. "Wait a minute," he said. "You said difficult, not impossible. Are you saying there's a chance he could be alive?"

Bookman shook his head. "No. I'm not. The remains we have are not conclusive, but the men went overboard in a place and a situation that doesn't support survival. Not only was the drill mechanism and a large diesel motor right there, practically beneath them, but as I mentioned, there were sharks, too."

Behind Zach, the groundskeeper pushed the cart that held Tristan's casket. One wheel was rickety and it creaked with every inch of movement. He turned.

Sandy, who was standing next to Duff, started

to turn around as well, but the priest kept his hand on her shoulder. With his eyes, he beckoned Zach.

"The Coast Guard has captured several of the sharks," Dr. Bookman went on. "They're sending me the stomach contents to see what additional remains I might be able to recover."

The queasiness rose in the back of Zach's throat again.

"Sorry about your friend," Dr. Bookman said.

Zach thanked him. He stepped quickly over to Sandy's side. He wanted to watch until the groundskeeper slammed the stone door and locked the bolt.

Actually, that wasn't what he wanted to do. He *wanted* to run over to the casket and rip it open. He wanted to see with his own eyes just exactly what was inside, if it wasn't his friend's body. But of course, he couldn't do that. He wouldn't. Sandy was there and he'd rather die than let her know that her husband's body was never recovered.

"Sandy," Duff said, "wasn't Zach one of Tristan's best friends?"

She glanced at him, not fooled for a moment, but allowing him to distract her from the sight of her husband's casket being pushed into the vault. "His *best* friend," she corrected, smiling at Zach.

He smiled back at her, and his conscious brain picked up on what he'd been aware of subconsciously since he'd first seen her. Sandy had always been slender, but the black dress she wore was formfitting and hugged a small but obvious baby bump. Tristan's widow was pregnant. His eyes burned and his heart felt broken into pieces. *Tristan had a child.*

Sandy's hand moved to rest on her belly protectively, and Zach realized he was staring. He looked up to see her smiling sadly at him. He opened his mouth to apologize or console her or something, but she shook her head. "It's okay, Zach," she murmured. "I'm doing okay. I'm about three and a half months along," she said, her voice quivering. "Tristan knew. He was sure it's a boy."

As he struggled for the right thing to say, he felt a presence behind him.

"Sandy," a voice said. It was the woman. "We need to get back to the house." She sounded exactly as he'd figured she would. She had a city accent. Maybe New Orleans, maybe another large metropolitan area. But one thing was for sure, it was certainly not a south Louisiana–bayou accent.

Turning, Zach met her gaze and saw for the first time that her eyes were blue. It didn't really surprise him. He didn't trust blue eyes.

Chapter Two

Her manner was no longer hostile, but it was decidedly chilly. Then she turned toward Sandy and within less than a heartbeat, her entire demeanor changed. A tenderness melted the ice in her eyes and her stiff shoulders relaxed. Zach shivered as the chill she'd aimed at him dissolved in the afternoon sun.

"You should lie down for at least a half hour while I put out the food and get ready for people to come by. Mrs. Pennebaker told me just now that she'd taken three more pies over and two buckets of chicken." She took Sandy's elbow and began to guide her away from Zach and Duff.

Sandy groaned. "How much do they think I can eat?" she said.

Zach was sure he'd heard a spark of amusement lighten her subdued tone for a second. Maybe she actually was all right. Or at least better than she looked, because she looked exhausted, crushed and on the verge of fainting, if he could tell anything by the paleness of her face.

"They know you're going to need lots of food, not only for yourself and the baby. Don't forget all the people who are going to be stopping by," the woman said.

"I know that. And I *don't* need to lie down. I'm fine." As the woman led her away, Sandy turned back, reaching out to Zach. He took her hand.

"Come by, please? We— I haven't seen you for such a long time. You're not leaving right away, are you? And bring your bags. You're staying with me."

Out of the corner of his eye, Zach saw the woman frown. That stopped the polite protest on the tip of his tongue. Instead, he nodded. "Thanks, Sandy. I'd be happy to." He shot the woman a sidelong glance.

"Oh, Zach, this is Madeleine Tierney," Sandy said, then turned to the woman. "I'm so sorry, Maddy. I forgot all about introducing you."

Madeleine Tierney nodded at him without offering her hand.

"This is Zachary Winter. He's Tristan's oldest and dearest friend, practically since they were born."

Zach nodded back at her. "I'll see you at the house, Sandy," he said.

As the two women walked away, he took a few seconds to study Madeleine Tierney. She had on a dark jacket and skirt that was a little loose. Her shoes were plain and black with a medium heel. Her clothes seemed designed to keep people from noticing her.

While she waited for Sandy to get into the passenger side of a rental car, she swept the dwindling crowd one more time. She spotted the two men she'd been watching earlier. Zach checked them out again, too. They were walking down Cemetery Road toward town. When they passed the last parked car, Zach narrowed his gaze.

"See those two guys, Duff?" he asked. "Oh, sorry, Father Michael."

Duff waved his hand. "Don't worry so much about what to call me. I'm fine with Duff, except in church," he said. "What two guys?"

Zach nodded toward the men walking toward town.

Duff squinted at them for a few seconds. "Oh. Right. That's Murray Cho and his son. Pat, I think is his name. Why?"

"Were they at the church service earlier?"

"I'm sure they were. I don't remember seeing them, though." He frowned at Zach. "What's bothering you?"

"Just wondering how they knew Tristan."

"From what I recall, when they first moved here, Tristan let them use his dock. They're small-time fishermen."

"Commercial?" Zach asked.

Duff nodded. "They bought the seafood-processing warehouse from Frank Beltaine. I'm not sure if they've gotten their commercial license yet, but they're working on getting freezers installed. I understand they're going to start selling to the locals soon."

So the two men were part of the community. If they just got started, they probably didn't have much money. Maybe they were walking because they didn't own a car.

Zach thought about Madeleine Tierney, who had fed his suspicion of the two men. "So, who is this Madeleine Tierney? And why is she yanking Sandy around as if she was an untrained pup?"

"She's not yanking Sandy around. She's been renting a room at Sandy and Tristan's for the past few weeks." Duff used air quotes around the word *renting*. "Since Sandy's been pregnant, Tristan was working more and more hours on the rig. He was spending two, three weeks offshore and sometimes only a week at home."

"Aren't there regulations that control how much they can work?"

Duff nodded. "Usually, sure. But I've heard

the rig is shorthanded right now because of some virus going around, and the crews can work overtime if needed. Tristan was trying to save money so he could quit offshore and go to work as a veterinary assistant. Madeleine and Sandy struck up a friendship and Tristan thought it was a great idea for Madeleine to stay with her because he didn't like her being there alone."

"So who is she and where's she from?" Zach asked.

Duff shook his head. "I understand that she's an oil rig inspector who's been—"

"A what?" Zach was stunned.

"An oil rig inspector. Her dad was an inspector until he retired. Seems like I kind of remember a kid going on inspections with her dad. But I never paid much attention to the oil rigs before the British Petroleum spill."

Zach nodded. He understood. Bonne Chance was like many of the towns and villages along the Louisiana Gulf Coast between Mississippi and Texas. The townspeople were a mix of fishermen and oil rig workers, and the two sides had a kind of love/hate relationship with each other. The oil rigs attracted big fish, including sharks, but they were a strain on the delicate ecosystem of the sea. Plus, everyone was supersensitive since the BP oil spill, which nearly wiped out the entire fishing industry along the Gulf Coast.

Zach hated the rigs. His dad had worked the rigs until the day he apparently got sick of work and marriage and took off when Zach was around eight years old, leaving his mother and him behind. Now a rig had taken the life of his best friend. It didn't matter that he hadn't seen Tristan in thirteen years. The hole left in Zach's heart hurt just as much as if they'd never been apart.

"Zach?" Duff said, drawing his attention back to the present. "I'll be at Sandy's in about twenty minutes, after I change clothes."

Zach nodded. Duff headed toward a new Mini Cooper. Zach turned his attention back to Madeleine Tierney, who was still hovering solicitously beside Sandy. She was looking up the road after the two men. As she watched them, she fiddled with the cross-body strap of the leather purse she carried. Something familiar in the subtle gesture, combined with the way she checked the clasp on the purse, stopped him cold.

He'd seen that exact set of gestures before. His weapons-training class with the NSA had included two women with whom he'd worked every day for twelve weeks. He'd watched them tuck their weapon into a specially made handbag and retrieve it time and time again. They had developed the habit of subtly locking and releasing the clasp of the bag, just as Madeleine Tierney was doing.

There was a concealed weapon in that bag. He'd bet a month's salary on it. He'd throw in another month's salary if carrying a concealed weapon were standard practice for rig inspectors.

Who the hell was she and what was her relationship with Sandy and Tristan? Judging by the bag and her handling of it, plus the way she'd kept an eye out for anyone suspicious, his guess was that she was a federal agent. Duff said she'd been here more than a month. Tristan had died five days ago, so she wasn't here because of his death.

Until he knew for certain who she was and why she'd gone to Tristan DuChaud's funeral packing a weapon, he wasn't going to let her out of his sight. She could be the key that would unlock the truth about Tristan's death. Even if that chance was one in a million, he couldn't afford not to take it. He'd stick with her until he knew everything about her.

He waited until she and Sandy drove away before he headed for his car, planning to follow them out to Sandy's house. But he stopped. No. There was one thing he needed to do first. He turned and looked at the grave site. Most of the people had gone. The casket was on a wheeled cart and the caretaker was just about to roll it into the open DuChaud vault.

Taking a deep breath, he walked over and asked the man if he could have a moment. The man stepped a few feet away. Zach bowed his head and put his hand on the cold metal of the casket. He knew it was empty, and yet it seemed appropriate to touch it as he said the only good-bye he might ever get to say to his oldest friend.

MADELEINE TIERNEY WAITED as the Cajun woman who had stayed at Sandy's house during the funeral fussed at Sandy. She turned the coverlet back on the bed. "Now you get under that cover, you," the gnarled little woman said. "And I'll tuck you in."

"I'm not sick, Marie Belle," Sandy had snapped irritably, but she lay down and let the woman tuck the coverlet around her.

Maddy had gladly stepped aside and let Marie Belle handle Sandy. Maddy hadn't had much luck convincing Sandy that she needed to rest for a while. On the other hand, even though Sandy argued, she listened to the little Cajun woman. And it was obvious by her pinched nostrils, pale face and sunken cheeks how exhausted she was. Her too-bright eyes were proof of the shattering grief that weighed her down, and the way her eyelids drooped was a definite indication that she needed a nap. She needed all the rest she could get, for the sake of the baby, if not for herself, Marie Belle told her. Meekly, Sandy agreed.

Meeting Marie Belle had given Maddy hope that she wouldn't have to deal with all the food that neighbors, friends and family had brought over. But no such luck. The Cajun woman needed to get home in time to boil a chicken for dinner.

Maddy told her to take some food with her, but the woman had shaken her head. "This food for Miss Sandy, yeah. T'ain't for me. You take care of that girl now. She needs rest."

Now, left alone in the kitchen, with Sandy resting in the master bedroom at the end of the hall, Maddy stared at counters stacked with pies, both homemade and bought, casseroles, bread and crackers and soft drinks and fruit. She opened the refrigerator even though she already knew it was full to bursting. She had no idea what she was supposed to do with all the food. She just hoped it was already cooked, because cooking was not her superpower. Sandy had taught her the basics of making scrambled eggs, but her best dish was still Marie Callendar's Fettuccini Alfredo with extra Parmesan cheese. The extra Parm was her special touch.

Cursing whoever had come up with the brilliant idea of sending food to mourners then showing up to eat it all, she checked the front door to be sure it was locked. She didn't want people coming into the house through two different entrances.

As soon as Marie Belle left, Maddy had gone into the guest bedroom and removed her Sig from her bag and placed it in the roomy pocket of her skirt, under the boxy jacket. An experienced law enforcement official or a seasoned agent might be able to tell that she was carrying a weapon, but it was unlikely that any of these folks could. She'd stowed her purse in the closet and headed back into the kitchen.

She was at a loss for what she could do to get ready for the onslaught of people who were on their way to Sandy's house. As she looked around helplessly, her thoughts went to the two men who'd shown up at the graveside service, dressed in clean, pressed slacks and shirts and yet looking out of place. Sandy had told her they were a local fisherman and his son, Murray and Patrick Cho. What bothered Maddy about them hadn't been their looks or their clothes. It was their attitudes that had worried her.

They'd avoided eye contact, seeming uncomfortable and yet almost defiant, as if they were expecting someone to ask them to leave. The son, Patrick, had stared at Sandy a lot. Once or twice his father had whispered something in his ear and Patrick had reacted with a sharp retort.

Thinking about them made her think about the other man who'd shown up at the graveside service but hadn't been at the funeral. The man with the sunglasses and the intense green eyes. She'd noticed him as soon as he'd taken his sunglasses off, while he was still standing next to his car. He was one of those people who command attention no matter where they go. He was tall, with dark hair and a lean runner's body. Just the type of body Maddy preferred in a lover. At least in a fantasy lover. She'd never dated a man with a body like that.

She blinked and shook her head. What had made her drift off into la-la land? She was on assignment—her first assignment. She hadn't anticipated that babysitting a pregnant widow and serving pounds of food would be part of the job, but she was a professional and she could handle anything that came her way.

Maddy glanced at her watch. Speaking of her job, maybe she had time to check in with her handler before all the people started arriving. She pulled out her phone. As she waited for Brock to answer, she spotted several stacks of red plastic cups someone had brought and left on the counter. She pulled one of the stacks toward her and twisted the tie that held the wrapper closed, but she couldn't get a good grip on it with one hand, so she stuck the package under her arm to hold it steady.

"Maddy, hi. How's it going?" Brock said. She knew very little about him, other than after military service he'd been in the CIA and had worked for an antiterrorist undercover agency for several years out in Wyoming after he retired from government service. She didn't know how he'd gotten from Wyoming to Washington, DC, or how he, as a federal retiree, could be working as a handler for Homeland Security undercover agents, but she did know she could trust him with her life, and that was enough.

"Hi. The funeral's over. That's the good news. The bad news is I have to be hostess for the entire town while they eat all the food they brought to Sandy's house." While she talked, she grasped the cups' packaging in both hands and tried to rip it, since she'd failed at getting the twist tie open.

"Right," he said. "You grew up in New Orleans. You ought to know Southern traditions," Brock said.

"I know them. I don't necessarily like them." With a frustrated grunt, Maddy ripped the plastic bag with her teeth. It tore straight down the middle and sent red cups rocketing across the kitchen island and onto the tile floor.

"Damn it," she whispered.

"What is it?"

"Oh, sorry, Brock. I was trying to open a bag of plastic cups and they just went sailing across the room."

"Do you have a report?"

"Yes, sir," she said, then took a breath. "Of course, I don't know everyone in town by name, but I do know their faces. I saw four people at the funeral that I'd never seen before." She bent over and snagged a small stack of cups that had landed right side up next to the refrigerator.

"Your assessment?"

"Sandy knew them. They were all members of the DuChaud family. She introduced me." Maddy rubbed her face and neck with her free hand. Tristan DuChaud's death hadn't left her unaffected. Although he was working undercover for Homeland Security just as she was, she'd never met him prior to coming to Bonne Chance.

After Tristan had reported that his cover may have been compromised and requested backup and protection for his wife, she'd been sent to arrange a spot inspection of the oil rig the *Pleiades Seagull* and slip him a secure satellite phone. But when she'd approached the rig's captain, he'd put her off, claiming a stomach virus outbreak making them too shorthanded.

While it left Maddy with her hands tied, it worked in Tristan's favor, as he could stay on the rig and work as much overtime as he could get, thereby having more time to eavesdrop on transmissions between the captain and his superiors and verify their conversations against the chatter the Department of Homeland Security had picked up about planned terrorist activity in the Gulf of Mexico.

It had already been established that much of the chatter originated from the *Pleiades Seagull*. On a rare week home with Sandy, Tristan had talked to his handler, citing several specific matches between unidentified chatter and telephone conversations that took place between the captain and an unidentified satellite phone.

His reports had prompted sending Maddy. By the time Maddy got there, Tristan was working practically nonstop aboard the rig. Once it was obvious that the captain was not going to allow Maddy on board, Brock had given her the alternate assignment of bodyguarding Tristan's wife, Sandy, cautioning her and Tristan not to let Sandy know that she was anything more than a new friend.

Maddy had been there nearly four weeks by the time Tristan finally got a week off. Between them, they'd convinced Sandy to let Maddy stay with her while he was working offshore. Tristan was happy because he wanted protection for his pregnant wife.

Maddy was not as happy. This was her first field mission and she wanted to be on the oil rig, in the middle of the action. She approached the captain a second time about a spot inspection. But again, he'd put her off.

Now Tristan was dead, and Maddy felt responsible. She blinked angrily at her stinging eyes. Stupid tears. She had always struggled with her weak side. The side of her that sniffled at funerals and weddings, and sometimes even Hallmark commercials.

"Maddy?" Brock said. "Continue."

"Right," she replied, blotting the dampness from her eyes with her fingertips, then grabbing for two cups that were slowly rolling toward the edge of the island. "There were fewer people at the graveside service. I saw three men who were not at the funeral. Two are Vietnamese fishermen, a man and his son, whom I had not seen before. Nor had I ever seen the third man." She stopped.

The third man. Once again, his image rose before her inner vision. His runner's body unfolding from the BMW. The sunglasses that he'd removed to reveal green eyes. According to Sandy, his name was Zach.

"Assessment?"

"Oh, right," she said, pushing thoughts of Zach out of her mind. "As I said, two of them were local fishermen, according to Sandy. Their names are Murray and Patrick Cho. They were respectful and dressed appropriately but seemed uncomfortable and somewhat belligerent, as if they were expecting to be grilled about why they were there."

"Did you get a photo of them or their vehicle? A license? Make? Model?"

"They didn't have a vehicle, at least not at the grave site. They walked back to town. And the entire time they were there, they didn't speak to anyone. They just stood and watched. A time or two they whispered to each other. Once, the younger one, the son, pointed at Sandy."

"Okay. Text me their names. I'll have them traced. What about the third man?"

"He was well-dressed and driving a BMW. I suspect it was a rental."

"So we can get ID on him."

"Absolutely. His name is Zachary Winter and apparently he's an old friend of Sandy's and Tristan's."

"Did you get a photo?"

Her hand tightened on the phone. "No. He was watching me the whole time. Sandy obviously cares a lot about him, but I don't think he's just a friend, though. He was too alert, too ready…"

"Ready for what?"

"Anything," she said as her imagination pitted Zach against a burly gunman, whom he took down with his bare hands as a single drop of sweat slid from his hairline down his temple. "I'm sorry, what?" she asked. Brock had said something else but she hadn't caught it.

"Text me his name and the license number of his vehicle."

"I don't have the tag. He parked too far away." She saw a car pass the kitchen window, then pull over and stop. "Oh, hold on. Maybe I can get it right now. He just pulled up. I can see the tag out the window, if I can just read all the numbers." She angled her head a bit so she could see the license and read it off to Brock.

"I'll see what I can come up with. You get all you can from him and Sandy DuChaud."

"Anything from your end? Are you going to be able to get another agent hired onto the rig?"

"It's not looking good. We're trying to see if we can go another way to find out what Tristan overheard and if it's an immediate threat. We may pull you out, based on what we find."

"Oh," Maddy said as another car pulled up to the house. "I'd like to stay," she said. "Sandy's pregnant and alone here." A third car pulled up. "Here they come."

"Who?"

"Everyone in town. They're all here to comfort Sandy and eat the food."

"Stay alert."

"No problem," Maddy said, resting her hand on her pocket, where she'd concealed her Sig P229 handgun. "I'm always alert."

"Usually," Brock said wryly.

"What? What do you mean by that?" she retorted.

"I thought I was about to lose you twice in this conversation. First with the cups and then again when you described the stranger who is *ready for anything.*"

"Give me a break, Brock. I was just reporting what I saw." She felt her face grow warm. "It's been a long day."

"Maddy, we don't know yet what we're dealing with. But you know that you have to assume that—"

"Everyone is a potential threat. I know. Don't worry. I've got this under control." She did. She was confident and alert. As confident as she could be. Tristan's death was unexplained. It could easily have been an accident, as the drilling company said. Accidents were unfortunately not unknown on oil rigs. But there was another possibility. A very real, very ominous possibility.

Two months before, Tristan had told his handler that the captain was becoming suspicious of him. That's when he'd asked for backup and protection for his newly pregnant wife.

"Brock? I know we have very little to go on, but what if Tristan was pushed or knocked out and thrown overboard? He was sure that the captain had found out he was listening in on his phone calls."

"The director is having that looked into, but it's a pretty touchy subject right now, with elections coming up. No congressperson is going to be excited about the possibility of corruption going on in the offshore drilling industry."

"But a DHS agent died," Maddy said.

"No. An oil rig worker died. We're not disclosing his connection to DHS. Not yet. The director is insisting on moving slowly. He's got experts reviewing all of DuChaud's communications for any clues."

"Clues? He told his handler he needed backup and protection for his wife. Isn't that a *clue*?"

"Agent Tierney, I have told you what the director's position is," Brock said coldly. Then he went on in a kinder voice. "Listen to me, Maddy. The director is concerned. He'll be speaking with the top officials of Lee Drilling, the company that owns the *Pleiades Seagull*, very soon. In the meantime, we need you to take care of Mrs. DuChaud."

"What about getting onto the rig?"

"No. That's no longer your assignment. We're trying out some new technology, advanced listening devices, to pick up communications on the *Pleiades Seagull*. So you don't worry about the platform."

"New technology? Why didn't you use those before, instead of putting Tristan in danger?" she asked.

"Carry on with your revised instructions, Agent. I've got a meeting."

"Brock?" she said, but the phone was dead. He had hung up. She picked up another cup and straightened, wincing at the disapproval in Brock's voice. He'd been in military environments throughout his entire career and he felt that interactions between officers and agents should be handled with a certain protocol.

When she looked up, Zach Winter was standing at the French doors. He let himself in. His jacket was slightly damp with sweat and a little wrinkled, as was the white shirt under it, but he wore them as if they were bright as the sun and freshly starched. His broad shoulders stretched the material slightly and the open collar of his shirt revealed a prominent Adam's apple and long, sinewy neck muscles that hinted at a serious and strenuous fitness routine. Her gaze moved to the perfectly fitted dress pants, under which were long, muscular runner's legs that complemented his lean torso and long arms. If he'd been a little thinner or taller, he might have looked awkward and rawboned. But he wasn't thinner or taller. He was just about perfect.

"Um, mind if I come in?" he said.

Maddy's gaze shot back up to his. Her face burned but she ignored it and gave him a haughty look as she walked toward him. Her foot hit a cup she hadn't seen. "Damn it," she said, bending down to pick it up.

At the same time, Zach did the same thing and their hands touched. "What happened here?" he asked. "Who detonated the cups?"

She suppressed a laugh and glared at him as she grabbed the cup away from him. She moved to rise and found that Zach was already standing, his hand held out in an offer to help her.

She ignored it.

"I'm Zach Winter," he said.

Maddy realized that as perfect as Zach Winter was, she didn't like him. Didn't like his attempts to be charming or his too-familiar demeanor. "Yes, I remember from Sandy's introduction," she retorted.

He nodded. "So are you called Madeleine, Maddy or Ms. Tierney?"

Sudden, swift anger bubbled up from her chest and tightened her jaw. She started to say that Ms. Tierney would work just fine, when someone else appeared at the door. It was Father Michael. "Hello, Madeleine."

Maddy cleared her throat and gave him a faint smile. "Hello, Father. I'm still hoping you'll call me Maddy."

"Well, all right, Maddy." He clasped her hand warmly as he glanced around the kitchen. "I see Zach and I are the first to arrive. Where is Sandy? Is she resting?"

Maddy nodded, then looked at the priest assessingly. "So, how do you two know each other?"

Father Michael raised a brow at Zach then smiled at her. "Let me introduce you to one of the most promising hometown boys ever to leave Bonne Chance. Zachary Winter. Zach, this is Madeleine Tierney." He smiled sheepishly. "Maddy."

Maddy met Zach Winter's gaze. His name fit him. It was sharp and cool, just like him.

"Sandy introduced us at the graveside service," she said. "Hometown boy? Odd that no one seemed to recognize you except the Father and Sandy."

Chapter Three

Zachary Winter looked at Madeleine Tierney blandly. "I've been gone a long time. Odd that you're so hostile toward me at our first meeting," he responded.

"All right, you two," Father Michael said. "Try to get along. I'm going to watch for other guests to arrive." He went out the French doors onto the patio.

"Not hostile," Maddy said. "Just curious. When did you leave Bonne Chance?"

He frowned at her, then looked away. "I was fifteen," he said shortly. "Can I help you round up the stray cups before they all get away? We can stack them and start putting ice into them and nobody will know they almost escaped."

"Ice. Damn it," she muttered under her breath. She'd forgotten all about ice.

Zachary Winter held up a glistening, dripping bag of ice. She hadn't noticed that he'd been holding it.

"Thanks," she said as people started coming in the door, directed by the Father. "There's tea in the refrigerator, if you wouldn't mind pouring it. And the water from the door dispenser is filtered. Thank you."

He walked around the kitchen island and set the bag of ice in the sink, then began scooping up cups from counters and the floor.

Maddy turned to greet the new arrivals. For several minutes, she was busy inviting people in and directing them toward the cups of iced tea and water Zach was setting out. Before she knew it, a small cadre of women had taken charge of arranging food on the island and counters so the guests could help themselves. Everyone was milling about with loaded paper plates and talking to each other.

She should have been able to breathe a sigh of relief. Obviously, these folks understood exactly how a wake went. But she couldn't. She'd been worried about Sandy for days, ever since they'd gotten the news about Tristan. Thank goodness she was resting finally. She'd hardly slept the night before, worrying about the funeral.

Maddy didn't want anybody—and she meant *anybody*—bothering Sandy, now that she'd finally lain down. It didn't matter what anyone's relationship was to Sandy, Maddy wasn't letting them past the kitchen.

She looked around for Zach and saw him leaning against the wall near the door from the kitchen to the hall. He looked relaxed, holding a glass of water and watching people as they ate and chatted. Every so often, someone would walk toward the door. When they did, he'd straighten and take a half step away from the wall, blocking the door. He'd smile and say something that made the other person smile.

There was something not quite genuine about Zach Winter. The phrase she used when she was talking to Brock was *too ready*. And that was it. He should have been like everybody else here, polite, subdued, a little shocked by the death of a vibrant young husband and father-to-be. But Maddy knew there was a lot more behind those green eyes than just a man who'd lost his best friend.

Zach Winter was not like anybody else here. He might look like a slightly bored young executive, sad about his friend but counting down the minutes until he could politely leave. But as she watched him, it hit her. He wasn't standing there because he liked the view.

He was *guarding* the door. Zach was guarding the door that led to Sandy's room. That's why her two-word summation of him had been *too ready*. She'd sensed it all along. It was in his deceptively casual stance, his bland expression belied by the sharp green of his eyes. He'd appointed himself guardian over Sandy.

So then, the question became, was he a concerned friend being protective, or was he, like she, something more?

At that moment, Father Michael said her name. After checking out Zach one more time, Maddy turned to the father. He had taken over as host and was greeting everyone at the door. He'd made it his mission to introduce her to each guest as they came in. It was a genuinely nice gesture, even if Maddy was tired of trying to keep up with the names of everyone in town.

After about a five-minute steady stream of people, Maddy excused herself and walked around the island to get a cup of water. But even there she found no refuge, because the women who were cutting pies into slices and dishing up casseroles were talkative, too. She smiled and nodded for a couple of minutes, which was all she could take.

She headed over to stand by Zach. "Hide me, please," she teased, then said, "Thanks for keeping people away from the hall."

Zach smiled, not even pretending he didn't know what she was talking about. "You looked nervous about the door, so I thought I'd help out by discouraging people from walking back there. But what do I tell them when they want to visit the bathroom?"

She gestured with the paper cup. "There's one in the laundry room. That door beside the refrigerator. Father Michael should be telling everyone when they come in."

"Oh, right. I remember that bathroom now. The ones who try to get past me want to 'peek in on Sandy.'" He checked the hall door to be sure it was latched. "How about Sandy. Is she asleep?"

"I doubt it, but she is lying down," Maddy said. "Hopefully, she's resting. She looked like she was about to faint by the time the graveside service was over."

"Sandy's a lot stronger than she looks," Zach commented. "Even pregnant."

Maddy blew out a frustrated breath. "I wasn't insulting her. Tristan asked me to be sure she was okay. I'm not sure she ever will be now."

"It's going to take her a while, but she'll be okay."

"Right. I guess I forgot who I was talking to."

"Pardon?" There was that quizzical smile again.

She gestured absently. "Tristan's best friend, right? Father Michael said you were born here."

He nodded again. After another swallow of water, he spoke. "Tristan's dad and mine were both offshore rig workers. My dad left us. Tristan's dad died as he was about to graduate high school. I hadn't talked to Tristan since we moved to Houston, but yeah." He paused and sadness clouded his eyes. "We were always best friends." He glanced over at her. "How much do you know about his death?"

She shook her head. "Not much," she said around a piece of ice she was chewing. "Almost nothing." *Stop*, she told herself. *Don't try too hard. Act like an ordinary citizen.* "It was an accident."

Zach's gaze had wandered, but it snapped back to her so abruptly that she was afraid for a second that she'd spoken aloud. "What about Sandy? Did she tell you what the authorities told her?"

"Some of it. I don't think they've told her much. Nobody saw what happened. The one thing that seems to have really devastated her is that they wouldn't let her see him."

Zach closed his eyes briefly.

"I saw you talking to the ME," she said. "You probably know more than I do. What did he tell you?"

"I just wanted to find out what happened."

She leaned closer. "He told you why they didn't open the casket, didn't he?"

He didn't answer her, but he didn't have to.

The tension in his jaw muscle, plus his silence, answered her. She suddenly felt queasy. "Never mind—" she started.

Just then, a short sound like a muffled shriek came from down the hall, in the direction of Sandy's bedroom.

"Sandy!" Maddy whispered and started to whirl. Immediately she caught herself, remembering that the people in the kitchen could see her. Damn it, she'd left her alone too long. She'd gotten caught up in trying to keep up with the guests, and then she'd gotten caught up in arguing with Zach Winter.

"What?" Zach asked, his voice low. "What's wrong?"

"I'll be right back," she snapped. "Close the hall door." She managed to walk steadily until she heard the door close, then she rushed to the farthest bedroom. She grabbed her weapon out of her pocket with her right hand and reached out to open Sandy's bedroom door with her left.

Just as her fingers brushed the curved metal of the doorknob, Zach stopped her.

"Wait," he whispered, his breath tickling her ear. She felt the heat of his body as he reached around to stay her hand on the doorknob. His right hand moved and she heard the unmistakable swoosh of gunmetal against leather and smelled the faint odor of gun cleaner.

"What are you doing?" she hissed.

"We need to be ready for anything," he said.

We?

"Get behind me. I'll go in first," he said.

"What?" Maddy's mouth actually fell open. "Are you kidding me?" She wrapped her hand around the doorknob. "You stand back," she commanded, grasping her weapon. "I'm a federal agent. DHS."

He went completely still, and cool air brushed her overheated skin as he drew away. "You're what?"

She thumbed off the safety and whispered, "On three. One, two—"

"Okay, Maddy Tierney. I'm a fed, too," he muttered.

The four words nearly knocked Maddy to her knees. She had to concentrate with all her might to stay focused on the danger that could be lurking behind the wooden door. "Three!" she barked and burst into the room.

Zach was in full-on SWAT mode, which was what he called the combination of tension and hyperalertness that hummed through him. He'd had the best training in the world. When the NSA had decided to oversee their own undercover operations, they pulled in the best of the best as teachers. Special Forces experts from every branch of the military. After all, they were training mathematicians, accountants and computer specialists to be warriors.

Zach followed Maddy through the door, still a little shell-shocked by what she'd said and newly surprised by what he'd felt when he'd reached around her to stop her from bursting through the door. He gave her the lead and backed her up the way he would any commander. There was no advantage in forcing the issue of who was in charge and no time to waste. He slid sideways, his back against the wall, and surveyed the darkened room, all his senses tuned to the slightest indication of danger. On the other side of the door, Maddy did the same thing.

The hyperalertness he'd cultivated during his training gave him the ability to divide his focus without sacrificing any of it. So, as he assessed the room, a part of his brain assessed Maddy. The tension radiating from her was so perfectly honed, so specifically focused, that it felt as though it was melding with his, turning the two of them into one perfectly functioning supersoldier. It was a stronger version of what he'd felt when he'd first seen her scanning the perimeter of the grave site, looking for any danger.

Everything from the slamming open of Sandy's bedroom door to this instant had taken less than three seconds, but Zach knew that lives could be lost in much less time than that. Just as his brain determined there was no immediate threat, Maddy motioned for him to stay put. She crossed the room and checked the windows. They were locked.

Zach looked past her out into the yard. The sun had gone behind the clouds again, turning the day dark and foretelling more rain. Less than a hundred yards from the house, where the lawn ended and the overgrown swamp began, everything was cloaked in gray mist.

Maddy glanced through the open bathroom door, nodded, then turned to the closet. She looked at Zach, then gestured with her head for him to back her up as she opened the door. He moved into position and held his weapon at the ready as she jerked the door open. The rows of men's and women's clothes were neatly hung, with shoes lined up on the floor. There was no place for a person to hide.

"Clear," she said.

He took one last split-second glance around and holstered his weapon, then turned his attention to Sandy.

She cowered against the headboard of the bed, her eyes wide as quarters and bright with tears. When Maddy walked over and turned on the bedside table lamp, Sandy squinted in the sudden light. She didn't seem to notice Zach and she stared at Maddy as if she were an alien.

"It's okay, Sandy," Maddy said. "It's okay."

"Maddy," Sandy gasped. "I saw someone at the window. A man, maybe two. They were looking at me."

"Two men? What kind of men?"

Sandy pushed her hair back with a trembling hand. "I don't know. Men." She glanced at the window and seemed to shrink back into the pillows.

Zach looked through the glass again. The day was getting darker by the minute. If there had been people at Sandy's window, they could have disappeared into the opaque mist with just a few footsteps. "I'll go out and check around the window for footprints," he said.

"No!" Maddy snapped. "Not now. Wait until the guests are gone."

"Why? We need to check for prints before it starts raining again."

"You'll alarm them and then word will get out and everybody in town will panic." She leaned toward him and lowered her voice with a quick glance at Sandy. "If she really saw somebody and it has anything to do with Tristan, we can't risk the people in town knowing."

"Yes, ma'am," Zach said sarcastically, even though privately, he knew that her argument made sense. Tristan's friends and relatives would probably riot if they thought there had been foul play involved in Tristan's death. He looked at Sandy. "Sandy, hon. Tell me exactly what happened."

Sandy frowned. "I don't know exactly. Something woke me, like a noise at the window. Once I was awake, I heard voices. The room was dark and I forgot—" She stopped. "I thought it was Tristan. Then I saw a face, or two faces, at the window. They were looking right at me, but when I cried out they disappeared."

"And it couldn't have been shadows, or a dream?"

Sandy turned to him. "Zach?" she said, looking surprised. Then with a hurt expression. "You think it was a dream?"

He held up a hand. "Just asking. Tell me what you saw. Did you recognize either of the men?"

She shook her head. "No. I—I don't think so."

Maddy stepped in. "What did they look like?"

"Dark," Sandy said. "I'm not sure. I didn't get a good look at them. Maybe foreign? At first it was just one. Then a second man came up. He looked angry. I couldn't see their faces because they were in shadow. Oh, I don't know," she finished, shuddering. "They were there and then they were gone."

"What do you mean by foreign?" Zach asked, thinking about the Chos.

Sandy looked miserable and confused. Zach felt bad about grilling her, but he needed to know whether she had really seen anyone at her window or if she'd dreamed it. Had Tristan's death put Sandy in danger? Or had it merely caused her to have night terrors?

"Did they have weapons?" Maddy asked.

"Weapons? Why would they?" Sandy's wide gaze stared at her then turned to Zach. For the first time, she noticed the weapon in his hand. "Zach, is that a gun you're holding?"

"Sandy, listen to me," Maddy said, holding up her gun for Sandy to see. "I have one, too."

Sandy recoiled.

"Sorry," Maddy said. She stuffed it into her skirt pocket and sat on the side of the bed. She took Sandy's hands in hers. "Don't worry. The only reason I have it is because Tristan asked me to keep you safe. We heard you scream, so we ran in here to check on you. Now, I want you to relax, okay?" she said gently as Sandy's fingers tightened around hers.

But Sandy wasn't comforted yet. She'd turned her wide, frightened gaze to Zach. "Zach? What's going on?" Her voice rose and her face seemed to grow more pale. "Does this have something to do with Tristan?"

Zach swallowed. "I don't think so," he said.

Maddy jerked her head toward the kitchen, an unmistakable order for him to leave. Then she turned back to Sandy. "You have guests," she said kindly. Do you feel like talking to them?"

"Window?" he muttered.

Maddy's eyes turned cold as glacial ice. "No. Stick at the hall door until everyone is gone. Tell Father Michael to say that Sandy will be out in a few minutes. Tell him to give her ten minutes to greet people, then he should start encouraging people to leave."

He was glad to be dismissed. Tears were flowing down Sandy's cheeks and he had never learned what to do when a woman cried. He was happy to let Maddy take the lead for now. She'd probably be a lot better than he would at calming Sandy down and finding out whether the shriek they'd heard was the result of a bad dream or something sinister. And she was right about the door. They needed to keep the well-meaning friends and relatives corralled.

He holstered his weapon and backed out of the room, closing the door behind him. As he did, he heard Maddy's voice, low and soothing. Her voice didn't go with the intensity she radiated. But he liked it. A lot. He wished he could thank her for being so sweet to Sandy.

As he turned around to head back to the

kitchen, he nearly ran into someone coming down the hall. "Whoa!" he said, holding out his hands.

"Oh!" the man exclaimed, but he didn't stop. He changed course, heading around Zach.

"Hang on a minute. Where do you think you're going?" Zach asked him.

"Hey, buddy," the man said warningly, then recognized Zach. "Oh, hey, Zach."

Zach looked at him more closely, trying to identify him. He looked vaguely familiar, but then so did about 80 percent of the people Zach had seen today. Bonne Chance was his hometown, after all, and in this part of Louisiana, a lot of people lived their entire lives less than ten miles from where they were born.

"It's Gene. Gene Campbell. I used to own the sports equipment store..." He paused with a shake of his head. "Until Walmart came to town."

Gene Campbell. He barely recalled him. "Right. Where you going, Gene?"

Gene stared at him, frowning for a few seconds. "Oh. You probably don't know. Sandy's my niece. Her mom died years ago, if you remember. I thought I'd check on her. Is she sick, or what? She ought to be out here with her friends and family." He tried to pass Zach again.

For a good ol' boy just wanting to check on his niece, Gene seemed pretty determined.

"I remember you, but no. I didn't know Sandy was your niece. I didn't think she had any relatives after her mom died. Didn't that elderly couple take her in?" Zach said. When Gene didn't seem inclined to answer, Zach continued, "Anyhow, we're trying to let her rest. She was pretty upset after the service."

"Oh, yeah? When I saw her talking to Father Michael, she looked okay."

"What's new with you these days, Gene?" Zach put an arm across Gene's shoulders and turned him back toward the kitchen. "How are the kids?"

Gene shrugged. "How long's it been since you been here? My kids are married and I've got three grandkids." He smiled. "They're the greatest gift in the world. How about you? Your mom doing okay?"

"Yeah. She's still in Houston. Doing great." Zach kept an ear trained on the bedroom behind him, but by the time he'd guided Gene back to the kitchen, neither Maddy nor Sandy had come out.

Just as Gene headed toward the kitchen island and the cups of iced tea, two elderly ladies peered through the door. "Is everything all right?" one of them asked.

Before Zach could answer, Tristan's mother scooted around the ladies. "Everything's fine," she said to them. "Don't you think we should put out more pie?" She smiled sweetly.

As the ladies disappeared back into the kitchen, fussing about which kind of pie would be best, Mrs. DuChaud tried to slip past him, but Zach calmly and gently blocked her.

"Oh, Zach, sweetheart," Mrs. DuChaud said. She held out her arms and Zach gave her a hug. She was plump and pretty, and her genes had given Tristan his good looks, but right now her face appeared to be melting. Her skin sagged and her eyes had big purple shadows beneath them. The muscles of her arms and back when he hugged her felt flaccid. "You're all grown up. And so handsome. But, dear, you should go see Ralph tomorrow and get that hair cut."

"Mrs. D. I'm so sorry about Tristan."

"Thank you. Excuse me, Zach, I want to check on Sandy." Mrs. DuChaud shook her head sadly. "She's just devastated. Of course, so am I, but I've got my faith and my friends to help me. Sandy, though. Well—" she shook her head "—I just don't know."

Zach winced at her implication. Mrs. DuChaud had always had a critical tongue. "Maddy is in there with her. She...had a bad dream and

Maddy's calming her down. She'll be out in a few minutes if she starts feeling better."

"Maddy? Oh. Madeleine Tierney. That woman. Who knows where she came from. But I thought I'd take Sandy a glass of water."

Zach double-checked her hands, but as he already knew, she wasn't carrying a glass. He raised his gaze and met hers without comment.

"I was going to ask her first," Mrs. DuChaud said. "I must say, Zach, you've changed since you left—how many years ago? You used to be such a nice polite young man."

"Yes, ma'am," Zach said dutifully, still blocking the door. After a couple of seconds, Mrs. DuChaud sniffed and turned on her heel.

For the moment, nobody else tried to storm the bastions, although a few people looked at him curiously and one or two spoke to him while eyeing the closed door behind him. Finally, he had a moment to think for the first time since Maddy had dropped the Homeland Security bomb on him. She was an agent for the Department of Homeland Security, he thought. Not much surprised him, but that had. It explained a little bit of what she was doing here. But why had she shown up several weeks ago? And had her presence here had anything to do with Tristan's death?

Just at that moment, Maddy and Sandy came

up behind him. He stepped aside as Maddy escorted Sandy into the kitchen, where it seemed as though half or more of the town waited to greet her and tell her how sorry they were.

With his new knowledge of her, Zach watched as Maddy guided Sandy through the cluster of people toward the ice water. She did a great job. She kept Sandy from having to say too much to any one person. Apparently, she was better at her DHS undercover job than at fixing and serving food and drink or handling a roomful of people. He smiled, remembering how nervous she was when he'd gotten there. She'd taken charge earlier like a veteran agent when she heard Sandy's cry of distress.

MADDY KEPT AN EYE on Sandy and was reassured by her steady stance and the way she greeted the guests. She stepped back to give the young widow the spotlight. Turning her head, she looked over her shoulder at Zach. He gave her a slight nod and she acknowledged it with nothing more than a blink as she walked across the kitchen to join him at the door to the hall. To the left of that door was another door that led to the hall from the living room.

Maddy looked at the two doors, then at Zach. Without a word, she knew he understood. The two of them would stand guard together, simultaneously watching Sandy and keeping anyone from wandering through the house unescorted.

She stood near the living room door, her feet slightly apart, her arms at her sides. She flexed the fingers of her right hand. Zach leaned against the wall about four feet from the kitchen door, his arms folded and one leg crossed over the other, as if he had nothing better to do than hang out for a few hours. Maddy realized he was listening to the conversations going on in the kitchen.

Of course, people were talking about Tristan and what a nice young man he was, and how tragic it was that his life was cut off so suddenly and uselessly. Inevitably, though, some conversations turned to other topics, like safety on oil rigs, the current state of the fishing industry compared to the oil industry, even high school football rankings and whether the Bonne Chance Gators had a chance of getting to the state championships.

But Maddy's thoughts remained on Zach. She kept replaying the four words he'd muttered just before they burst into Sandy's room. *I'm a fed, too.*

"So what you said back there about being a fed, too. Just what did you mean?" she asked.

Zach was leaning against the door facing in his usual relaxed manner, his arms crossed. He didn't move, not even his head, but he sent her a sidelong glance. "You want to talk about that now?"

Maddy rolled her eyes. "Yes. Why not?"

"Just thought you would rather discuss it in private."

"I'd rather know who I'm talking to. I knew you were carrying the first time I laid eyes on you, but I need to know who you work for." She spoke in a low voice while she watched Sandy. "She's doing really well," she added.

"What? Oh, Sandy. I told you she's strong. I knew you were armed, too."

"Really? How?"

"That purse. You acted just like the female agents I trained with, fooling with the lock and keeping your hand on it."

"Okay, maybe I'll ditch the purse." Maddy rubbed her eyes. "Sandy may be strong, but she's also exhausted and grief-stricken. She hasn't slept since Wednesday, when she got the news about Tristan," Maddy said.

"Maybe she'll sleep tonight, now that she's—" He stopped.

"Now that she's what?" She glanced at him. "Buried him? Is that what you were going to say?"

He looked a little stunned. "Uh, no. I mean,

yeah. That was it." He rubbed his face and squeezed his eyes shut for a second.

"You know, we almost didn't have a funeral. Sandy was extremely upset when they wouldn't let her see him," Maddy said.

"Well, you know why, right?"

"No. I figured maybe there were some, you know, injuries."

Zach stared at her. "Really? You don't know?"

"Look. I saw you talking to Dr. Bookman. He wouldn't talk to me. Did he tell you anything?" Zach had been here only a few hours and he'd managed to find out something she'd missed.

He shrugged.

"Oh, come on. Just tell me so I'm up to speed." Her face and neck felt hot. It wasn't easy for her to admit she'd made a mistake. That she'd missed something. But the sooner Zach shared his information with her, the sooner she could be back on track. And nothing—certainly not a strong, handsome federal agent—would be able to knock her off her game again. She made a vow to herself that nothing and no one, not even Zach Winter, would distract her from her assignment.

"You don't know why they wouldn't allow her to see anything or let her have an open casket?"

Maddy saw the grim expression on his face.

She took a deep breath and blew it out slowly. "Tell me," she said.

"The ME told me there weren't enough remains to put in a casket. The little bit they found was placed into evidence. Tristan DuChaud's casket was empty."

Chapter Four

Tristan's casket was empty. Maddy shuddered. "Oh, no," she said. "Poor Sandy. You can't tell her."

Zach's face went dark. "*You* can't tell her. And I swear if you do, I'll hang you up and skin you like a deer. Do you understand that?"

"Of course," Maddy said solemnly. "What else did he say? Did he have any word on cause of death?"

"Nope. No cause of death. Speculation is that he fell into the water from one of the lower metal catwalks. They said he and the Vietnamese guy with him may have gotten into a fight or were roughhousing or were drunk and fell overboard."

Maddy was shaking her head before he finished speaking. "That's not Tristan," she said.

"I know that, but how do you know that?" Zach's voice was low-pitched and toneless. The deadly seriousness of it made her shiver.

"Sandy told me. She's been in a bit of a haze ever since she found out about his death. She hasn't asked very many questions, but when Father Michael came to talk with her and told her some of what you're telling me, she said Tristan would never have fallen. I only met him twice during his weeks off, but I agree. He apparently lived here and boated and swam and climbed around the trees and the cypress roots all his life. I don't think he would have fallen, either."

"You're right. That's exactly what I said when the ME tried to sell me on the idea that he fell. Tristan would never have fallen off the platform. He was pushed."

Maddy stared at him as she ran the past few seconds over in her head. *He was pushed.* "That's it," she said. Her hand flew up to cover her mouth and tears filled her eyes. "That's it," she repeated sotto voce.

"What?" Zach snapped, frowning at her.

"It's the only thing that makes sense. He was pushed." She grabbed his arm. "And when Sandy starts thinking straight again, she's going to realize that. Oh, poor thing. How is she going to deal with that? With the fact that Tristan may have been murdered?"

Zach stood and started pacing. "If I have anything to do with it," he said through clenched teeth, "she won't have to, because before she figures that out, I'll have all the answers and we'll have whoever killed him *and* whoever ordered it done behind bars. Sandy won't have to face that unknown. She can at least have the comfort that the person who killed Tristan will be punished."

"You think you can do that? Okay. I think it's about time you told me who you are and who you work for," Maddy started, then realized she had raised her voice and a few people had turned to look. She smiled and cleared her throat, then spoke out of the corner of her mouth. "Please just tell me."

Zach blew out a frustrated breath. "I thought we ought to wait, but fine. I work for the National Security Agency, as an undercover agent." He pulled a badge holder from his back pocket and handed it to her.

She took it and glanced at it, then did a double take. After a few seconds, she looked up at him. "The National Security—" Her voice cracked. She stopped and took a deep breath and tried again to speak. "You mean the NSA? You work for the NSA?"

Zach's gaze narrowed. "That's right. The No Such Agency. Yes."

"But you're— You've got a gun." Her surprise morphed into incredulity.

"Try not to sound so impressed," he said wryly.

"But why? Why do you have a gun?" she

asked, spreading her hands as if imploring him to explain. "I mean, okay. You're here because your friend died, and I know that you're concerned about Sandy. But really? What's up with the NSA? I thought they were all accountants and math whizzes, not undercover agents."

Zach scrubbed a hand down his face. "I'm a member of a division of the NSA that investigates possible terrorist activity, based on information the NSA gains from its listening activities. But I am on vacation right now. I'm not here in any official capacity. I'm just Tristan's and Sandy's friend."

Maddy stared at him for a long time, until he began to feel extremely uncomfortable. He rubbed his face again and was just about to ask her if he'd grown a third eye when she finally spread her arms again, palms out.

"So you're telling me you work *undercover* for the National Security Agency and you're licensed to carry a gun?" Maddy asked as her brain fed her a picture of nerdy guys in ill-fitting suits and taped-up glasses wielding guns.

"That's what I'm telling you," he said. "Want me to go over it a third time?"

Maddy shook her head. "No. I've got it. NSA," she said and chuckled without much mirth. "Who knew the No Such Agency was in the 007 business?" She shook her head. "So, what are you by profession? I'm guessing not a career soldier."

He lifted his chin. "I have a double PhD from Harvard. Math and forensic accounting."

"Ohh," she said on a chuckle. "Math and accounting. And how much experience have you had as an undercover agent?"

"Not much," he admitted, his jaw muscle flexing. "I've been on one mission, which turned out to be some kids that had hacked their favorite MMO game and changed all the villains' names to real terrorist names."

"MMO game?" she parroted. "I don't know what that is."

"MMO stands for Massive Multiplayer Online game." He waved a hand. "Don't worry about it. As I said, I'm not here in an official capacity." He looked at her. "Are you?"

Maddy ignored his question. "NSA undercover agents. Now I've heard everything."

"You've heard everything?" Father Michael said. "How about telling me some of it, because I believe I've still got a lot to learn."

"Oh, Father, you startled me." Maddy hadn't noticed him until he'd spoken.

"I just wanted to check with you before I go. Sandy is trying to make me take all the food with me." He nodded toward the kitchen counter where Sandy was packing up food in shopping bags. She looked up and smiled wanly.

"Good, because there is no way we will ever eat all that."

"Thank you, Madeleine—I mean, Maddy, for taking care of Sandy. And you," he said, turning toward Zach. "You keep these two women safe, you hear me?"

"Don't worry, Duff. I plan to," Zach said. Father Michael left, loaded down with food, and Maddy locked the French doors behind him. She sighed in a mixture of relief and exhaustion and rested her forehead against the door for a couple of seconds.

"Maddy, are you okay?" Sandy asked.

"Sure," Maddy said, turning around and smiling tiredly at her. "So," she said to Zach. "You call Father Michael Duff?"

"Can't seem to get used to Father Michael." He turned to Sandy. "Why don't you go back to bed? You can sleep late in the morning."

A faint shadow crossed Sandy's face. "I'm not sleepy," she said, then turned her attention to Maddy. "You're the one who needs to go to sleep. You look absolutely exhausted. Zach and I are just going to visit for a while."

Maddy looked at Zach, who gave her a brief nod. "Okay. I could use a shower. Maybe I will go to bed early, since Zach is here."

"Good. You've taken such good care of me. I appreciate it." Sandy held out her arms and Maddy hugged her briefly.

"You're sure?"

"Of course. I'm going to make up the Hide-a-Bed sofa in the nursery for you," she said to Zach. "Then we can visit. But first, I've got to pee, *again*. Apparently, when you're pregnant, the peeing never stops. Not even for a *funeral*." She stalked off down the hall.

Zach looked startled. Maddy looked at him. "That was a joke. Maybe she's doing better. Before she gets back I want to ask you something," Maddy said. "Do you believe what she said?"

"You mean that she saw someone at her window? I have no idea. I don't know anything about pregnant women. Are nightmares or delusions common?"

"Don't ask me," Maddy snapped. "But you know her. So, do you believe her or not?"

"I believe she believes there were two men there. Do I think she actually saw two men sneaking around and looking in her bedroom window while there was a houseful of people here, including the sheriff? No. Not really. What about you?"

"That's pretty much what I think, too. But what if they were there? Who were they? What were they doing?"

"That's what I'm asking you. What about those fishermen you were watching so closely. Could it have been them? Does Sandy know them?"

Maddy frowned at him. "I suppose it could have been the Chos, and yes, she should have recognized them. But why would they be sneaking around the back of the house?"

Zach shrugged. "Why were you so suspicious of them?"

"Suspicious?" she repeated. "I was keeping up with everyone at the funeral service and the grave site. They weren't at the funeral service." She paused for a second, assessing him. "Neither were you, as a matter of fact."

He nodded without speaking.

"I actually can't imagine the Chos sneaking around Sandy's house, and I can't imagine Sandy not knowing who they were."

"Maybe she was half-asleep. Or completely asleep and the men at the window were nothing but a dream. What if it were a couple of oil rig workers? Maybe they knew Tristan and came to the funeral."

She shook her head. "One, if they were oil rig workers, they'd have to be off duty this week or they were sent by the captain. Two—" she held up two fingers "—if you work on an oil rig, you don't just ask for the afternoon off, grab a boat or order a helicopter and run over to the mainland. You should know this. Your dad worked on a rig, didn't he?"

Zach scrubbed a hand down his face. He was tired and he didn't want to talk about his family or his childhood in Bonne Chance. "He did, but he left when I was eight. I didn't know anything about oil rigs. All I knew was that he was gone most of the time and when he was at home, neither he nor my mom were happy."

"And three, as I told you, I kept up with everybody who came to the funeral and the graveside service," she finished. "There were no oil rig workers there. And if I missed someone, then Father Michael missed them, too. He paraded everyone who showed up past me and even though I don't know all their names, I did recognize them all."

It occurred to Zach that Maddy's knowledge of the oil rigs was good to have. Maybe he did get why DHS had sent her and why they'd hired her in the first place.

"I don't know," he said with a sigh as he heard the door to Sandy's bedroom open. "We need to take all this one thing at a time. If it's okay with you, after I talk Sandy out of making up that sofa bed, I'll go out and check for footprints. I'm afraid it's going to start raining again."

Maddy smiled as she arched her neck and

massaged it. "Sure," she said. "Why are you asking my permission?"

He snorted. "Are you kidding me? You told me in no uncertain terms that you are in charge here."

She eyed him with a raised brow. "You're telling me you're ready to take charge now?" she teased.

Zach felt as though her gaze were singeing his skin. He swallowed and shifted slightly, surprised that his body was straining in reaction to her teasing words. For someone who was not his type, she could take him from zero to uh-oh in no time flat. He forced himself to speak lightly, with no trace in his voice of the struggle he was waging to keep himself in check.

"Madeleine Tierney," he said. "When I'm ready to take charge, believe me, you will know it." Then he turned and headed down the hall to the nursery, where Sandy was waiting for him.

"I'LL NEVER UNDERSTAND GUYS," Sandy said, setting a stack of sheets and pillowcases on the back of the sofa. "How can you still be best friends when you haven't spoken for over a decade?"

Zach shrugged. "We're guys," he said, then peered at her closely. "Are you okay, Sandy?"

She smiled sadly and shook her head. "No.

How can I be okay? He's dead. I don't remember a time when he wasn't here—" She stopped and blotted a tear that was sliding down her cheek.

Zach nodded. "I know. I can't believe he's gone, either."

Sandy swiped at another tear, then frowned at him. "You two were arguing the night before you left."

"Not really arguing. It was just guy stuff."

"It was about me. Tristan acted jealous, but he never really believed I would cheat on him. But he did not like that you and I talked."

Zach smiled in recollection. "He was afraid I'd tell you all his secrets."

"And I want to thank you for doing that. I knew how to handle him because of the things you told me."

"You needed to know. Tristan is—was—a hardheaded idiot at times." He stumbled over the present tense and Sandy heard it. Her lower lip quivered.

"I'm so sorry you and Tristan never talked after you left," she said.

"Trust me, it was no big deal. I told him he ought to treat you better—treat you like his girl-friend, not another buddy to hang out with. I said if he didn't, he was going to lose you."

"Oh, Zach. That's why he slugged you, isn't it? What did he say?"

Zach's mouth curled into a smile. "He agreed with me."

"Agreed? But he split your lip."

He nodded. "Like I said, he agreed with me."

Sandy laughed. "He never liked being proven wrong." She started to reach for one of the sofa's seat cushions.

"Don't do that," Zach said. "I'll be perfectly comfortable stretched out here on the couch."

"It's no trouble," she said, reaching forward and trying to grasp the corner of a heavy seat cushion.

"Hey," he said, "stop that and sit. I need to hear all about this baby." He *needed* to hear all about the supposed accident that had killed his friend, but he wasn't going to make Sandy talk about that.

"And I need to hear how your mother is, and Zoe."

Zach sighed. "Mom's fine. She blossomed in Houston. She got a job at a big department store and is now one of the buyers, and she's become a total fashionista. She's a local celebrity because of her fashion style."

"Wow," Sandy said, her brows raised. "Double wow because you know the word *fashionista.*"

Zach laughed.

"How's Zoe?"

His laughter faded immediately. "I haven't heard from her in a couple of years. Last I knew she was in Atlanta. She was married for a short while—I'm talking months. Mom said she's thinking about moving to New Orleans. I can't imagine why."

"Poor Zoe. Fox Moncour's death that graduation night really changed a lot of things in Bonne Chance, didn't it?" She paused. "I'm worried about how Tristan's accident will change things. I'm not sure I can stay here if the town takes his death as hard as it took Fox's."

Zach studied Sandy. Her gaze was on her fingers, which were playing with the corner of a pillowcase. He wanted to ask her how sure she was that Tristan's death was an accident, but he couldn't do that to her. Not on the day of her husband's funeral.

IT WAS TWO HOURS later when Sandy went to bed and Zach went out to examine the ground around Sandy's window. As he'd predicted, it had started sprinkling rain, not hard enough to wash away footprints, but still, he hadn't found anything. The grass under the window was too lush and thick to show footprints.

In the nursery, he eyed the seven-foot-long sofa that was supposed to turn into a bed with just a tug on a lever. He'd told Sandy he would be just as comfortable stretched out on it.

Right now, he felt as if he could sleep on nails, he was that tired. He grabbed one of the pillows Sandy had brought him and tossed it at one overstuffed arm.

He turned the lights out and began unbuttoning his shirt. He'd hoped to talk to Maddy some more, but she and Sandy had both been visibly exhausted. By the time he'd come inside from checking out the window, they'd gone to bed.

He was tired, too. As he'd explained to Sandy, his return flight was on Sunday, leaving New Orleans at 7:05 a.m., which meant he had to drive back to New Orleans tomorrow. She'd been disappointed and her eyes had gleamed with tears, but she'd smiled and told him she understood.

He flopped down on the sofa and stuffed the pillow behind his head, then threw an arm over his eyes and tried to relax. He wanted to get up early and spend some time with Sandy as well as talk to Maddy before he had to leave.

He had a method he used to get to sleep when he was too keyed up. He began to breathe deeply and slowly. Starting at his toes, he deliberately relaxed one muscle group at a time, moving up his legs and torso and out his arms to his fingers, then his neck and head and eyes. Usually, no matter how wide-awake he was, he'd be asleep before he got to his neck, sometimes before he got to his arms.

But within moments, it was obvious that tonight, his brain had no intention of slowing down. He managed to doze, but within seconds, some disturbing thing someone had said about Tristan would echo in his head and wake him up.

The first time he drifted off, it was his own voice, telling Duff that Tristan couldn't have fallen into the water and drowned. *Tristan lived on boats and docks and floating logs on the Mississippi River and on the Gulf his whole life. He was the strongest swimmer I've ever seen.*

By the fourth time, he'd barely fallen asleep, only to wake to the echo of the ME's horrifying statement, *There's not enough of Tristan DuChaud to put in a casket.* He gave up and sat up.

There was no way he could sleep. Not until he sorted out all the information in his head. He needed to think, therefore he needed to pace. The nursery didn't have enough room for him to take two steps back and forth, much less four or five. So he maneuvered around the baby bed in the middle of the room and quietly opened the door. Slipping out and up the hall to the kitchen, he ran a glass of water and drank it, then started to unlatch the doors to the patio and stopped. There were two tiny metallic plates between the top of the door and the door facing that he hadn't noticed before. It was an alarm. Obviously, it was not armed, because it didn't go off when he came in through the door, nor had the sheriff come roaring out to the house, called by a silent alarm.

He glanced at the window over the sink, then checked the front door. It appeared that all the doors and windows were armed. He remembered noticing a box on the wall behind the door between the hall and the kitchen earlier in the afternoon. He looked at it. Sure enough, it was the control for the alarm system, and it was off. Not just disarmed. Off. He made a mental note to check that everything worked and to make sure Maddy and Sandy knew how to arm and disarm it before he left for New Orleans.

He opened the French doors and slipped through them onto the patio, then closed them as quietly as he could. The air smelled like rain and the humid breeze on his skin felt a lot cooler than the steamy afternoon at the cemetery, although he'd be surprised if it was any lower than midseventies. He rolled up his sleeves and let the air pick up his shirttails.

For ten minutes or so, he paced and ran his fingers through his hair, rubbed his face and slammed one fist into the other palm as he went over everything he'd learned in the short time he'd been here.

Finally, he came to a conclusion. There was only one thing he could do, for Sandy, for himself and for Tristan. There was no way he was leaving in the morning. He sat down at the picnic table and dialed a familiar number.

"National Security Agency, how may I direct your call?"

Zach gave the operator the name of his immediate superior.

"Yes, sir. Just a moment, sir." He listened to the subtle beeps and clicks as she transferred his call.

He yawned. It had been a long day. He'd flown from Fort Meade, Maryland, to New Orleans, then driven over three hours to get to Bonne Chance. He'd barely had a chance to breathe before finding out the horrifying specifics of Tristan's death. He'd parried with Madeleine Tierney and helped her when Sandy screamed, and he hadn't even stopped to eat a sandwich or a piece of pie. And now it was midnight here, one o'clock in Fort Meade.

He doubted Bill was still at the office. He probably wasn't even awake. Sure enough, the voice that answered was dull with drowsiness.

"Yeah?" Bill said.

"It's Winter. I need a favor," he said. He heard bedclothes rustle as Bill sat up in bed with a groan.

"A favor?" Bill asked. "At one o'clock in the morning?"

"I need to take some vacation time."

"Vacation—that's what you called about?" Bill's voice was no longer sleepy. It was annoyed.

For an instant, Zach considered telling Bill everything he'd learned and everything he suspected. But he didn't. He knew what would happen if he mentioned Homeland Security to Bill. He'd be pulled back to NSA headquarters, and Bill would start a turf war with the Department of Homeland Security under whose purview chatter fell. So he gave Bill the story he'd decided on while pacing.

"My friend Tristan's wife is pregnant and she needs me to help her with his papers. You know, insurance and accounting stuff." Zach cringed at his lame reason. "I'd have to leave in the morning to make my Sunday-morning flight, so I wanted to check with you about staying a while, maybe a week or—"

"Yeah, yeah. Send me an email. I'm sure I won't remember this when I wake up. And just so you know—you could have arranged this before you left."

"Yes, sir."

"Good night."

"Good night, sir."

Bill hung up. Zach quickly typed an email and sent it, formally requesting the next five days as vacation.

MADDY WAS PRETTY sure she'd never felt so tired in her life. She'd spent a long time in the shower, letting the hot water run on her back and neck, her arms and body and, finally, her face. It was only when the water turned cold that she got out. She wrapped up in a terry-cloth robe, her limbs rubbery and her eyelids drooping.

By the time she'd gotten a pair of camisole pajamas on, she'd been more than half-asleep standing up. But as soon as her head hit the pillow, her brain started racing. Each time she began to doze, her brain kicked into high gear. Zach's voice hammered at her consciousness. *Who are you? Who do you work for? What happened to Tristan? Does Sandy know? What happened to Tristan? What happened? What—*

She sat up and clapped her hands over her ears, but since his voice was in her head, it didn't help. Why was she hearing Zach's voice asking questions he'd never asked her? She didn't know why, but inside her head he was relentless. Lying back down, she closed her eyes and pulled the covers over her head. That didn't help, either. Now that she'd covered her head, it wasn't just Zach's voice. Her handler Brock's voice echoed through her brain, too. *You're not focused. We may pull you out.*

"Shut up!" she whispered, sitting up. "Shh." She'd heard something. She held her breath and listened. It was a door closing. Two doors, like the French doors out to the patio. It wasn't Zach coming in from checking Sandy's window. She'd heard him earlier, before she'd gotten into the shower. Could it be Sandy?

She waited, but didn't hear anything else. If it were Zach or Sandy, getting a glass of water, wouldn't she be able to hear the water running? Maybe not, if the water were in a filtered dispenser on the outside of the refrigerator.

She got up and reached for her gun, but at that moment, she heard Zach clear his throat. Then she did hear the water running. It was Zach, and he was getting a glass of water, probably wearing nothing but his underwear, given the weather. No, she couldn't go out there. She didn't think she could bear to look at that body of his in nothing but briefs or boxers.

Pressing a hand over her racing heart, she lay down again and closed her eyes—tightly. What was the matter with her? Now her head was filled with a vision of Zach Winter practically naked, drinking a glass of cold water. He turned it up and guzzled it, and of course, a few drops escaped and ran down his chin to his neck, to his torso, to the waistband of those briefs—or boxers.

She moaned and moved her hand from her heart to her temple. Pressing hard, she tried to squeeze the Zach fantasy out of her head.

Brock was right when he said she seemed to lack focus. And from the way he'd said it, he suspected that Zach was the reason.

With a low growl, Maddy threw back the covers and got up. She hoped and prayed Zach was back in his room with the door shut, because if she ran into him in just briefs or boxers— well. Before that thought had a chance to finish, Maddy was shaking her head. She was *not* going to let a good-looking NSA agent knock her off her game. This was her first field assignment and she intended to ace it.

Despite her resolve, it took her a few minutes to decide to open the door and peek out. The door to the nursery was closed. Did that mean he'd sneaked back in without a sound? Or was he still out?

She slipped up the hall to the kitchen and got herself a glass of water. As she drank, she saw a dark form pacing back and forth on the patio.

Her heart didn't quite jump out of her chest because she was pretty sure it was Zach, but she did stand perfectly still and watch, until she saw his face and body in a small patch of moonlight that peeked out from the clouds for a few seconds. She exhaled, having totally failed to notice that she wasn't breathing until that moment.

Then she stepped over to the door and opened it. Without the windows between them, she was able to see him a little more clearly, especially after her eyes adapted to the darkness. He wasn't undressed, but he had unbuttoned his shirt. When she saw that, her heart did jump out of her chest, or at least it felt as if it had. Then she opened her mouth and, because she'd made herself nervous thinking about his naked body and couldn't take her eyes off his bare chest and abs, she said something snarky and mean. "So, Zach," Maddy said. "Texting for a booty call?"

She grimaced, then nearly turned and ran when she saw him close his eyes in brief but very real pain. "In the home of my best friend's widow, on the day of his funeral?"

"Oh," she moaned aloud. "I'm sorry. I don't know where that came from. My evil twin, I suppose."

"Really?" His jaw worked. "Are you telling

me that I've been talking to the *good* twin up until now?"

"Okay, I deserved that. I apologize. I didn't mean to say what I did. I was just—" She shrugged.

"Just what?"

"So, what are you doing?" she asked, trying to sound as if the prior exchange hadn't taken place.

"I'm not going to tell you."

She smiled and shook her head. "Can't blame you. Would it help if I answered some of those questions you said you had for me?"

His brows rose. "Maybe," he drawled. "What are you doing up anyhow?" he asked.

She saw his gaze take in her state of dress—or undress. The camisole pajama set she had on covered enough, she supposed. At least in the strict sense. But the material was thin cotton and although the top was dark blue, it still showed the shape of her nipples. She crossed her arms instinctively. Then when he smiled, she uncrossed them, felt exposed and crossed them back immediately.

When his gaze slid farther, down to the drawstring bottoms, she was thankful at least that they were long and not the short-short ones she'd started to buy. As his eyes lit on her feet, she had to force her toes to stay still and not curl in the pink flip-flops she wore.

"I was thirsty," she said, trying to pretend he wasn't checking out every inch of her. "And I was having trouble sleeping."

"Counting those sheep didn't help?" he asked, nodding toward her pajama bottoms, which had white fluffy sheep bouncing around on the same dark blue background as the top. She shrugged. "Guess not."

ZACH PERCHED ON one hip on the corner of the picnic table as he slid his phone into his back pocket. Then he went back to studying her. He'd already checked out the little pajamas and decided they were very sexy. He didn't even pretend that he wasn't ogling her body. He was too fascinated with the way the dim light from the kitchen played across her smooth, creamy skin. He was mesmerized by the little shadow created by the small bump of bone on the top of her shoulder. For one instant, he had the notion that it would be fun to chase that shadow—with his tongue.

He squeezed his eyes shut. He couldn't think of her that way. She was a Homeland Security agent. He wanted, needed, to find out what happened to his best friend. There was no place for sex here. No place even for just a flirtation.

Besides, there was almost nothing about her that he actually liked, except maybe that little shoulder bump. She was too confident, too sure of herself, too bossy, and she wasn't even that pretty. Okay, that wasn't fair, or true. He'd already decided that she was quite attractive, although not without flaws. She had nice hair, but her eyes were too big and her nose was too short and her mouth was too...something. Maybe too turned down at the corners? Maybe too pouty. Although, he had to admit that it was tempting. Very inviting.

He realized he was staring and she was becoming uncomfortable. His gaze lit on her right hand. Her fingers were drumming on her thigh. When she noticed him looking at her hand, she stopped and made a fist. He tried not to smile. He liked that he got to her. "You're an interesting person, Maddy," he finally said.

"So I've been told. Why do you think so?"

"How old are you?"

She took a long breath then sighed. "Is that what you wanted to ask me?" she said. "I'll just go back to counting sheep."

"At the funeral, in that dark suit, I'd have said thirty."

Maddy's jaw dropped before she had a chance to cover her surprise. "Well, I suppose I ought to be glad."

"Glad?"

"I dress that way on purpose, especially when I go on the oil rigs. It's easier if the guys think I'm older."

"I guess that makes sense. But right now, it's hard to believe you're not still working on your PhD." He tried not to smile.

"I have my PhD, thank you."

"In what?" he asked.

"Chemical engineering."

He nodded. "And you work for Homeland Security."

"Yes. Just like I told you."

"Why are you here?" he asked, folding his arms.

"Because I was assigned as backup for Tristan."

Zach went stone-cold still at Maddy's words. He had to play them over in his head more than once before he was sure what she'd said. "Backup," he repeated flatly.

"Oh. I'm sorry," she said, her face turning pale as her cheeks turned bright with color. "I didn't mean to blurt that out. You didn't know Tristan was working undercover on the *Pleiades Seagull* for the Department of Homeland Security, did you? I didn't mean for you to find out like this."

"Tristan, working for the government? That's

not like him. And it sure as hell isn't like him to work on an oil rig. I remember he hated the oil rigs and that was back before we were in high school, before his dad died on one. Does Sandy know that you and he were—are with Homeland Security?" He rubbed his palm across the evening stubble on his face.

"I don't know," Maddy said. "I mean, no. I don't think so. She doesn't know about me. I'm pretty sure she doesn't know about Tristan. I can't tell you why he went to work for them. Maybe he was recruited because of where he lived and his particular skill set. They like to hire locals." She sighed and lifted her hair off the back of her neck, then shivered.

"You said you were sent here as backup for him? Why you? Did they send anyone else?"

"First of all, thank you," Maddy said wryly. "But no. I was sent because I'm an oil rig inspector. The plan was for me to conduct a spot investigation of the *Pleiades Seagull*, which, as an inspector, I'm allowed to do at any time. However, the captain of the rig can refuse if he has a good reason."

Zach didn't want to hear all this. All he wanted to know was what happened to Tristan and whether it was Homeland Security's fault. He wasn't sure what good it was going to do him or Sandy or anyone to know that, but right now, having that knowledge was the only thing that mattered to him. He gritted his teeth and tried to ask the right questions to get to the answers he needed. "I take it the captain of the *Pleiades Seagull* refused?"

Maddy nodded. "He stated that he was short-handed because several crew members had contracted a stomach virus."

Zach looked out into the darkness toward the Gulf. A pale glow lit the sky from the oil rigs and boats on the water. "Why are you hanging around here now?" he asked.

"My secondary assignment was to protect Sandy. When Tristan requested backup, he also requested protection for her."

Zach whirled and grabbed Maddy's arm. "Protection? He asked for protection for his wife? That means he *knew* he was in danger. He *knew!* Why the hell did Homeland Security leave him out there alone?" He let go of her and pressed his temples with the heels of his hands, feeling as if he'd been kicked in the head. "If they knew Tristan was in danger, why didn't they pull him out?"

Maddy hugged herself. "I asked that same question. My handler, Brock, didn't answer me directly, so I have no idea what their plans were. But they did send me in. I was supposed to stay with Sandy and make sure Sandy was safe and let Brock know about any information I received from Tristan. It was only going to be another week or so before he'd have been back on shore for a week and DHS could find out his latest information and decide what to do."

Zach felt a lump growing in the back of his throat and his eyes were stinging. "Nice plan. How'd that work out for everybody?"

Chapter Five

Maddy's chin shot up and she glared at him while tears spilled from her eyes and flowed down her cheeks. She dashed at them angrily with her fingers. Her cheeks turned such a bright red that he thought her tears might sizzle and evaporate. "You go right ahead and be derisive and sarcastic. It's not going to make one bit of difference to me. I am fully aware that Tristan was killed on my watch. I will never—" Her voice cracked. She cleared her throat. "Never get over that. I should have been able to do something, even from here. I should have realized that he was too vulnerable out there on that rig alone."

She wiped a strand of hair away from her forehead with a shaky hand. "I should have called headquarters and made them get him off there."

"Would they have listened to you?"

"I don't know."

"Were you and Tristan able to talk while he was offshore?"

She shook her head. "No. Sandy didn't know that either of us was with Homeland Security, and Tristan had been caught eavesdropping on the captain twice. All I could do was listen in on their conversations and glean what I could from Tristan. He knew that the captain had his phone bugged from that end and that I was listening on this end. We had hoped that he could give me some carefully worded clues while he talked to Sandy, but we also knew that if it was a clue I could understand it would probably make sense to the captain of the *Pleiades Seagull*."

Zach's jaw was still tight. "That doesn't sound like a very good setup."

"It was a horrible setup. After the captain refused to let me on board to do an inspection, I was helpless, except as a bodyguard for Sandy. I even went back after three weeks and asked him again, hoping he'd be more cooperative. But he still refused." Her voice cracked.

"If he'd agreed in time, you think you could have saved Tristan?"

"I don't know. Maybe if there really was a virus on board, I could have forced the captain to evacuate the boat and fly everybody to the hospital in New Orleans. That way we'd have at least been able to get to Tristan and possibly remove him from danger, instead of hanging him out to dry."

"Is Homeland Security sending someone else to work on the rig in Tristan's place?" Zach demanded through clenched teeth.

"No. They have no way of getting another agent on the platform. The oil companies like to hire locals, preferably people who are already familiar with the rigs, but they'll take someone who has worked and lived on the coast of Louisiana all their life. From what I understand, Tristan was already working as communications officer on the *Pleiades Seagull*, so he was literally the perfect recruit for an undercover operation."

"Until he was murdered." Zach wasn't sure how much longer he could control his emotions. The more he heard, the more convinced he was that Tristan's death could have been avoided. He could still be alive, loving his wife and waiting for his first child to be born. Zach turned and looked out over the Gulf. He didn't say anything. Not because all his questions had been answered, but because he didn't trust his voice right now.

After waiting in silence for several moments, Maddy finally spoke. "Okay, so, I'm going back to bed, unless you've got more questions."

"Wait," he said, his voice raspy with emotion.

For another half a minute he stood there, his back to her, trying to regain control. He hadn't seen Tristan in thirteen years, but he still felt as though a part of his heart had been ripped out. They'd been best friends throughout their entire childhood.

Finally he turned around. "Listen. I'm supposed to fly back to Fort Meade on Sunday, but I've asked my boss for a week's leave." He looked down, wishing he were stronger and braver. "I'm not sure why I did that. I have no authority. I'm just a government employee on vacation. Anything I do will be as a civilian, not as an NSA agent."

Maddy felt deflated. She'd hoped, one way or another, that she could convince Zach to help her figure out a way to bring down the people who had killed Tristan. She'd hoped he would talk to his superiors at NSA and they would get involved. Because she knew that all Homeland Security wanted from her was protection for Sandy. And Brock had hinted that they would probably be pulling her back to DC very soon.

She blew out a breath in frustration. "I don't get it. Why did you ask for vacation? Why didn't you tell your chief what's going on and request assignment down here? That would have made more sense."

Zach rubbed a hand down his face. "Because

first, I can't prove that Tristan's death was foul play. All I've got is what I know about him. Second, the NSA is not in the business of solving murders. And third, even if they did decide to investigate Tristan's death, I wouldn't get the assignment. I've never been in the field before. I just finished training a few months ago. And last but maybe most important, I was Tristan's best friend all through childhood. That's a conflict of interest."

"So you decided to take a week's vacation? Why? Are you planning on going rogue?" Maddy felt laughter rumbling up into her throat. She tried to hold it back but she couldn't.

"I'm sorry," she gasped. "I don't mean to laugh. I'm just tired."

He glared at her, but she was right. It was kind of funny. Maybe he was *going rogue*, he thought, but he discarded that notion right away. He could call it that, but it didn't make it so. All he was really doing was planning a little amateur detective work while on vacation. He wasn't like some Special Forces officer in a movie who couldn't get permission to go back into enemy territory to save his friend.

He was a geek. His weapons were two PhDs and a gun he barely knew how to use.

"Laugh all you want. You're not much better. You're babysitting Sandy. Not that I don't appreciate you keeping her safe. But why are they leaving you here? Obviously you're not going to get onto the *Pleiades Seagull*."

"I'm planning to talk to my handler about that first thing in the morning. I need to report to him about the men who were supposedly peeping in Sandy's window anyway."

"Come on, Maddy. How long do you think they're going to keep you here to guard Sandy now that Tristan is dead? The only reason they would is if they had any proof—" He stopped, cocking his head to listen.

"Wha—" she started, but he held up a hand, signaling for silence. He was suddenly as still and alert as a cat on the prowl. He lifted his head as if sniffing the wind.

Then she heard it. Someone, or some*thing*, was moving stealthily through the swampy area at the back of the house. The muffled footsteps and faint rustling of leaves and vines were subtle, but once in a while she could hear the sucking sound of a leg being pulled out of the sticky gumbo mud that made up the swamps of south Louisiana.

"Get down!" Zach snapped, grabbing her arm and pulling her down with him behind the picnic table. She lost her balance and fell on her butt, then scrambled up to her haunches.

He pulled his weapon out from the holster

nestled in the small of his back and held it in both hands pointed skyward as he listened.

"What—" Maddy started, but he shook his head jerkily. She crouched there beside him, close enough to his left arm that she could feel the heat and the tension emanating from him in waves, and waited for whoever was sneaking around Tristan and Sandy's house to show themselves or slink away. She heard more movement disturbing the quiet air. She held her breath. The sounds were fading.

"Are we going after him?" she whispered, her mouth close to his ear.

This time the shake of his head was slow and deliberate. "No," he said finally. "I don't want to ask for trouble, either of the two-legged or the four-legged variety."

"Four-legged? You think it was an animal?"

He shrugged. "Stay down," he said as he rose slowly, still listening, still tensed and ready for anything. Maddy did her best to ignore the hint of rippling thigh muscles that were beneath the fine weave of his dress pants, right in her field of vision. *Long and lean and hard.* A shiver rippled through her.

What was she thinking? From the moment she'd first set eyes on him, all the practical sense and excellent intuition that made her a good rig inspector and a good undercover agent had blown away like dandelion spores on the bayou breeze. What had replaced her focus and single-minded determination was a searing fire deep within her, like lightning striking a methane swamp. She'd been shocked at her girlish response.

Thank goodness her training and personal determination kicked in when Sandy had cried out. She'd handled that well, even during those two or three seconds when Zach had leaned against her and stopped her from opening the door. The feel of his hot skin against hers and his breath on her cheek had registered but not distracted her from her mission, which was to keep Sandy safe.

But just moments ago, when she'd seen Zach on the patio with his shirt undone, she'd gotten swept up in the fantasy of him again, despite the fact that she knew as clearly as if he'd told her that she was not and had no hope of ever being his type.

Gathering every ounce of will she could muster, she pushed the feminine side of her to the back of her mind and forced herself to react like an agent, not like a *girl*.

"So," she said as she rose and eyed the blackness at the edge of the lawn that was the swamp. "What was it? A dog? An alligator?"

He stood, still and silent, for a few more seconds, still holding his gun at the ready, then he clicked on the safety, holstered it and turned to face her. "Dogs aren't generally that stealthy unless they've been trained. Alligators make a different sound."

"It sounded big."

He looked at her, one brow quirked. "Aren't you from New Orleans? And didn't you tell me you'd gone everywhere with your dad? You're not trying to say you've never been in the swamp, are you?"

She shook her head. "Nope. Never have. Never will—not on purpose anyhow. So, let's see. Maybe possum?"

Zach laughed. "Right. Try nutria, coyote or bear or bobcat."

"Bear? B-bobcat? Seriously? Are *they* stealthy?"

"Okay. Maybe not the bear."

Maddy groaned. "Great. So it's a zoo out here, only the animals aren't locked up." She expected Zach to laugh or at least chuckle, but he didn't. He gave her a solemn nod.

"Neither the four-legged kind nor the two-legged kind," he said. "So it might be a good idea if you keep that gun on you at all times."

There it was. The subtle reprimand she'd been expecting. She was on assignment and she'd walked out onto the patio unarmed. Her face flamed even as a chill crawled down her spine. "Right. Now what?"

"I'm going to bed. I've had a long day."

Zing. Another not-so-subtle slam. She should have beaten him to that punch. She should have said she was going to bed first. She kept relinquishing power to him when there was no need to. He'd already acknowledged her as commander at the door to Sandy's room.

"Sure. Me, too. I'm tired." She turned and headed inside, not waiting to see if Zach was behind her. About the time she got to the door from the kitchen to the hall, he spoke.

"Maddy?"

She stopped. "Hmm?" she said without turning around.

"Can I talk to you for a minute before we go to bed? I want to run something by you."

She looked back over her shoulder. "Now?" she said, faking a yawn, only to have it turn into a real one. "Can't this wait until tomorrow?"

"Nope. And close that door. I don't want to wake Sandy."

"Are we going to yell?" Maddy closed the door and turned, wondering what he had in mind. He stood right in front of her, his shirt still open. His abs were tight and rippled with muscle the way those of male models in commercials and book covers were. She'd always suspected those photos were touched up.

A thrill zinged through her and seemed to

flip a switch deep inside her. She felt a sensuous throbbing in a very, very sensitive place. She took a deep breath and reminded herself that she wasn't his type.

He sent her a look that told her he knew exactly what was going on in her head and elsewhere. Again, her cheeks grew hot. Ducking her head, she went to the refrigerator for a cold glass of water. She took several swallows before she turned around to face him. She had to resist the urge to press the cold glass against her burning cheeks.

"Okay," she said briskly. "What can't wait until tomorrow?"

He leaned against the wall near the door to the living room, crossed his arms and slanted one calf across the other. It was a deceptively casual stance. But Maddy, after only a few hours with him, knew that nothing about Zach Winter was casual. Not his words, not his demeanor and certainly not his stance. She was sure that underneath those perfectly tailored pants, the leanly sculpted muscles of his thighs and calves were taut and ready. If he had to, he could vault across the room in a fraction of a second and pull his gun while he was doing it.

"I don't like Sandy being here."

"What?" Maddy asked, thrown off guard by the statement. "Why not?"

"There's no reason she needs to stay here. She'd probably be happier up in Baton Rouge with Tristan's mother. It would probably be good for both of them. Mrs. DuChaud could use someone to fuss over and Sandy could use a distraction. She'll be more comfortable there."

"Because you're all about Sandy's comfort, right?" Maddy set her jaw. "What's going on, Zach?"

He just shook his head and leaned against the wall, lanky and carefree as a farmer after his last harvest.

"Come on. You take a week's vacation to stay down here, and the first thing you do is send Sandy away? What are you planning?"

He still didn't speak.

"Okay. I could be in bed, except that you said you wanted to talk to me. So, why aren't you talking?"

ZACH STRAIGHTENED AND STUCK his hands in his pockets. He looked down at his feet for a second then up at her. "Okay," he said. "I think Sandy is in danger. That's why I don't want her here. She's pregnant, she's grieving and she has no training in self-defense. She'll just be in our way."

"*Our* way?" Maddy echoed.

Zach ignored her. "You and Sandy are similar in height and your hair color is pretty close. Here's what I'm thinking. Let's say the doctor orders Sandy on bed rest for the rest of her pregnancy and says that she's having some kind of problem that not only confines her to bed but also quarantines her for her health and the health of her baby."

Maddy frowned at him. What he was saying began to make sense, but she didn't like what she was pretty sure he was getting at. "I don't understand."

"I want to get Sandy out of town secretly and put you in her bedroom, pretending to be her."

"You want to use me as *bait*?"

Zach shrugged. "I wouldn't put it that way, but if that's how you want to look at it…"

"It's not how I want to look at it," Maddy said. "It's how it is. You're putting me in Sandy's room in Sandy's bed, pretending to be Sandy. The definition of that is *bait*." She stood and smothered a yawn with her hand. "I think I'm fading. When are you thinking about doing this?"

"The sooner the better."

"Please tell me you're not wanting to do it tonight."

He shook his head. "I'm not sure I could do it tonight, even if I wanted to. But I'm going to have to talk Sandy into it and I can guarantee you she's not going to like it. So maybe we should regroup tomorrow."

"That works for me," Maddy said. "I'm really tired."

"So, I guess I'll see you in the morning."

Maddy looked at her watch. "Hate to break it to you, but it's already morning. It's 3:00 a.m. I'll see you in a few hours."

"Where are you sleeping?" he asked.

She thought of a cute, slightly suggestive response, but she couldn't work up the energy to say it out loud. Besides, it would probably only end up being embarrassing if it went the way her previous attempts to be cute and sexy usually went. "In the guest room," she said.

"Why don't you sleep in Sandy's room. I saw a daybed in there."

"Why? Are you thinking—"

He nodded. "I'd like one of us to be there with her, just in case anything happens."

"So, have you decided she wasn't just having a nightmare when she saw those two men at her window?" Maddy asked, searching his face.

"I think it could be dangerous to dismiss what she says she saw," Zach said grimly. He walked over and opened the hall door. "So I'll see you in a couple of hours."

"At least three," she said, yawning. At that instant, out of nowhere, came a high-pitched scream.

Maddy jumped and Zach drew his weapon. "Get your weapon and meet me in there. Approach with caution."

Zach vaulted through the open door at a run and headed toward Sandy's bedroom at the end of the hall. He heard Maddy's footsteps behind him and noted when she veered off into the guest room to grab her gun. He stopped at the edge of Sandy's door, holding his weapon in his right hand, supported by his left, just as he was taught. He knew he could shoot. He also knew he was not very good at it.

And he had no idea whether he could shoot a human being. Still, his gun was ready, safety off. He took a deep breath and decided that he was ready, too. As ready as he'd ever be.

He reached for the doorknob with his left hand, exhaled, then twisted the knob and shoved the door open.

The room was dark, very dark. He stood totally still, poised on the balls of his feet, prepared to dive, lunge or shoot, whatever the situation called for. He felt a fine trembling just beneath his jawbone. Praying he wouldn't lose his nerve, he felt behind him for the light switch, braced himself, then turned the lights on. The flash blinded him for a split second and left a red spot glowing in the middle of his vision.

Sandy's back was pressed against the headboard and her eyes were wide as saucers. One hand was pressed against her throat as if to stop more terrified screams.

Holding his weapon at the ready, he crossed the room, glancing briefly into the closet and the bathroom, and looked out the window. Nothing but blackness. He held his breath and listened. The only sound was the faint dripping of water off the trees and the house's roof.

As Maddy slid into the room, brandishing her gun, Sandy cried out, "Maddy! Maddy— Oh, my God, Maddy! I saw him."

"Zach?" Maddy said softly, the tone of her voice a clear indication that this time she was looking to him for leadership.

He nodded. A second later, he heard the quiet whoosh of a metal weapon being slipped into a leather holster. Then Maddy was on the bed and cradling Sandy in her arms.

"Who did you see, Sandy? The same men?" Maddy's voice was low and soothing. He was grateful that she was here. He wasn't sure how bad he would be at comforting his best friend's widow, but he knew he would be bad.

"No!" Sandy cried. "I thought it was them—

at first—but it wasn't. Oh, Maddy! It was him. He was right there."

Zach carefully lowered his gun and slipped it into its holster as he watched Maddy slowly and gently calm Sandy down. It took her a while. At first, Sandy didn't want to be calm. She wanted to get up and run outside, or at least that's what Zach thought she was saying.

After a little while, her excited cries gave way to mumblings, which he couldn't understand at all. During all that, Maddy held her and whispered to her. Zach just stood there and watched until Maddy caught his eye and pointedly glanced toward the window.

Zach nodded. She was right. He needed to go outside and look around. It didn't take him long, and once again, he saw nothing. The thick grass under the window wasn't even bent.

When he came back into the master bedroom, Sandy was crying less and talking more coherently. Maddy still had her arm around her and Sandy was staring into space. But Maddy's penetrating gaze caught Zach's eyes and bored into his brain. She wanted him to listen. He stopped and waited.

"It really was, Maddy," Sandy said. She held a couple of tissues in her hand and kept wiping her eyes with them. "It really was him."

"Sandy, you're so tired, and there were people

here until after eight o'clock. You probably heard them and they kept you from sleeping well. It's exhaustion. Did the doctor give you something to take if you can't sleep?"

Sandy shook her head and Zach saw her chin lift fractionally. He knew that look. She had no intention of letting Maddy or anyone else stop her from telling what she saw. "I saw him. I did. Oh, he looked awful."

She pulled away from Maddy and looked Zach in the eye. "Why is everybody telling me that Tristan is dead, Zach?" she asked, her eyes overflowing again with tears. "When I woke up a few minutes ago, he was standing right there."

Zach held up his hand. "Maddy, would you get her some water?"

Maddy nodded and got up. She turned toward the bathroom.

"From the kitchen," Zach added.

"Zach—" Sandy sobbed. "He was there, alive. Smiling at me."

But she wasn't smiling. Her face held a puzzled sadness that was about as painful as anything Zach had ever seen.

"He was soaking wet and so pale. He looked awful. I held out my arms for him but he disappeared. He must have had to hide, because one of those other men showed up at the window." She shuddered. "I think I screamed."

"Start at the beginning, Sandy. I need to know exactly what happened. What woke you up?"

Sandy relaxed a bit and pulled the covers up to her armpits. "I was lying here awake. I know I was awake because I was thinking about the funeral and how everybody had insisted on keeping the casket closed." She stared at her hands.

Zach saw a tear splash onto her thumb. He felt as if he should do something. Hug her. Wipe her tears. Something. But all he did was wait, silently, for her to continue.

"He was standing right over there." She pointed to the window. "Like I said, he looked awful, but then I guess he's been through a lot."

Zach's eyes burned. He needed to stop her, to tell her that she'd been dreaming, that she couldn't have seen Tristan because he was dead. He didn't have the heart. Hell, he could barely stand to think about Tristan, much less have to convince his wife—his widow—of something he didn't want to believe himself.

But if not him, then who? Not Maddy. She was a stranger. He'd known Sandy for almost as long as he had Tristan. He had to be the one to comfort her, no matter how badly he botched it.

With courage he pulled up from somewhere deep inside him, Zach sat down on the bed. He held out an arm and Sandy moved closer. He slid his arm around her and pulled her to him so she was resting her head against his shoulder. "Sandy, sweetheart. We've known each other longer than anybody, except for Tristan and me. And you know you're my sister, as truly as if we had the same mother."

Sandy's shoulders shook with her tears. "I know. I love you, Zach."

"I love you, too, sweetheart. I need to tell you something. It's going to be hard for you to hear, and I'm going to do a really bad job of it, but you're strong. I know you can handle it."

At the word *hard*, Sandy looked up at him, fear and trust in her eyes.

"Go after him, Zach. He's out there, wet and cold and exhausted. He might even be hurt. Find him and bring him home to me. Please."

From the corner of his eye, he saw a movement in the doorway. It was Maddy with a glass of water in her hand. Zach inclined his head toward the front of the house, sending her a message to leave them alone. She set the water down on a table by the door and disappeared.

Zach pressed his lips to Sandy's bowed head as he blinked against the sting of tears in his eyes. "I need you to be brave."

Sandy went rigid, except for her hands, which trembled against his skin. "I don't want to be brave, Zach," she said. "I don't want to."

"I'll hold you," he said. "I'll hold on to you."

"Okay," Sandy said so softly it was nearly inaudible. "I'll try."

He pulled her closer, terrified at the trusting way she'd looked at him. His stomach was in knots and his eyes were blurry with dampness. He thought this might be the hardest thing he'd ever done. He'd sooner take a bullet than tell her the whole truth about Tristan's death. But she deserved to know.

He took a long breath. "Let me tell you what happened to Tristan," he said gently.

Chapter Six

Maddy stood frozen, just beyond the bedroom door. She couldn't leave until she'd heard what Zach was going to say. When she heard his heartbreaking words and Sandy's brokenhearted reply, she rushed into the guest room and closed the door quietly behind her.

She stood with her back against the door for a long time as Zach's gentle words to his best friend's widow echoed through her over and over, etching another scar onto her heart with each pass.

She doubled her fists and pressed them against her chest. She could barely breathe, the pain was so fierce. Tears coursed down her face and neck, drying before they reached her pajama top.

After a long time, she wiped the tears away with tissues, but even though the crying stopped, the pain in her heart still throbbed, more intense than anything she'd ever experienced.

"How?" she asked aloud. "How can anyone stand that much hurt and live?" She was talking about not only Sandy, but Zach as well, and she felt as though just knowing how much they were hurting might suffocate her.

Sandy's husband, her soul mate, the father of her unborn child, was dead, and she had to go on living. How would she do it? Maybe she could stand it, for their baby. The baby would give her joy and heartache, blissful happiness and aching grief. After more than a month of living with her, Maddy knew that Sandy would survive. She was strong. She and her child would be all right.

Maddy dried the last lingering tears. She wondered if Zach would want to talk to her after Sandy went to sleep. She could stay up—maybe, if she made a pot of coffee—or she could try to go to sleep. Zach would probably have no qualms about waking her if he needed to talk to her.

Climbing into bed, she picked up one of the pillows and hugged it. She had a different view of Zach after what she'd seen him do. She couldn't imagine doing that, not even for her best friend. He was telling Tristan's wife the whole truth about what had happened to him.

It seemed at first blush like a cruel thing to do to Sandy, when she was already so devastated. But it was obvious Zach was doing the right thing. The look on Sandy's face told Maddy that he was doing the right thing.

Maddy's tension began to drain away as her mind followed Zach's reasoning. Years ago, he'd known Sandy almost as well as he'd known Tristan, she realized. And so he understood that she'd spent the days since Tristan's death in terrified confusion because no one would explain why she was being kept from seeing her husband's body. No one, not the medical examiner, not even Father Michael, had had the nerve to explain why.

Maddy's eyes welled with tears again. She swiped at them with her fingers, remembering the glimmer of dampness in Zach's eyes as he gestured for her to leave them alone. Zach was doing what a true friend did. He was helping Sandy to understand.

The sharp, cool NSA agent had a tender side, a side he would not want her, or anyone else, to see. He was a man, and men didn't weep. Not even over the death of their best friend.

But if he thought she wouldn't respect him for grieving, he was wrong. He didn't know that she'd seen her father crying over her mother's grave when she was eight years old. Zach didn't know that Maddy had learned that a man who would not cry was a man who could not feel—not the way he needed to in order to be a great leader.

Maddy turned over on her side, still hugging the pillow. Tears slid over the bridge of her nose and down onto the sheets. Sandy was truly lucky to have Zach in her life.

Just before she drifted off to sleep, Maddy thought about what her life would be like if Zach were in it.

FOUR HOURS LATER, Maddy came into the kitchen, freshly showered and wearing jeans and a sleeveless top. Her eyes were still puffy and she had a faint headache that she was hoping a couple or three cups of coffee would fix.

To her surprise, the coffee was made and smelled delicious. She looked out at the patio and saw Zach sitting on the far side of the picnic table with his back to the door, drinking coffee. He was facing the swamp.

She poured a mug for herself, added three heaping teaspoonfuls of sugar and headed outside. This morning she was carrying her weapon in the pocket of her jeans. As she stepped onto the patio, she saw Zach's gun sitting on the table next to a towel he'd used to wipe last night's rain off the table.

Without speaking, Maddy dried the table on the other side of his weapon and sat. She drew in a deep breath scented with mud and fish and seawater, then took a long swallow of her coffee. "Mmm," she murmured appreciatively.

Zach acknowledged her presence with a slight incline of his head before he drained his mug. Then he rose.

Maddy suddenly felt desperate to keep him there. She didn't want to sit out here alone with her thoughts. She wanted to talk to Zach. Wanted him to tell her that Sandy was just fine after he'd told her about Tristan. She wanted to hear that Sandy had agreed to go to her mother-in-law's house and leave the two of them here to battle whoever had killed Tristan, if anyone even had. "Don't go," she said, sounding pitiful.

"More coffee," Zach said gruffly, brandishing his mug as he hoisted himself up and headed for the house.

"I mean," she amended, clearing her throat, "come back, will you? Once you get the coffee? I want to—" She paused, trying to decide what to say. "—catch up." *That was lame.*

She half turned and saw him nod. With a sigh, she turned back around and watched the birds chase each other as she sipped her coffee. By the time Zach got back, she'd finished all but the last swallow. Instead of sitting on the bench, he climbed up and sat on the table with his feet on the bench beside her. He had on running shoes and old faded and frayed jeans that fit him in that perfect, comfortable way old jeans did.

Maddy leaned back against the table. "How's Sandy?" she asked.

"Okay." Zach's voice was still gruff. Maddy couldn't help but wonder if he'd slept any better than she had.

"You ended up staying with her all night, didn't you?" she asked. "Because I figured you'd have called me if you needed me to sleep in there. You're a wonderful friend."

He didn't answer.

"Is she going to go to her mother-in-law's? I mean, did she agree to?" she asked.

"See for yourself. She'll be up in a minute. I heard her moving around in her room just now."

"Oh," Maddy said, standing. "I'll start breakfast for her. She'll need to eat." She looked up at him and caught him staring at her. She knew her eyes looked swollen and bloodshot. She squeezed them shut for a second. "I hope my eyes aren't as red as they feel," she said. She took a good look at him. His eyes were red, too.

"I don't think they're as red as mine," he said, his gaze moving to the inside of his mug. "They look fine."

"Do you want some eggs and toast?"

He darted a look at her then back to his mug. "So you can cook now? Seems like it was just yesterday that you couldn't put ice into plastic cups."

She sent him an irritated look. "Sandy has taught me a few things since I've been here. How to make coffee and cook scrambled eggs. I already knew how to use a toaster."

He nodded sagely. "How about sausage or bacon?"

"None of that in the house," she said. "The smell makes her queasy."

"Okay. Eggs and toast it is." Zach stood and hopped down from the picnic table right in front of Maddy. He looked down at her with an odd expression on his face. "Thanks," he said.

Maddy turned to head into the kitchen. "Are you ready to eat now?" she asked over her shoulder. When she turned to look at him, she saw he had his cell phone out.

"Soon as I make a call," he said, then, "Damn. What's wrong with the service around here? I got a signal last night in the nursery."

"I think Tristan put in some kind of booster or something in the house. You may have to make your calls in there."

Maddy got out the eggs and bread from the refrigerator. She wasn't much for breakfast. Coffee sustained her until lunch and sometimes until dinner. But since she'd been here she'd been eating a piece of toast while Sandy ate her eggs.

During the past week before they got word of Tristan's death, Sandy had been having less morning sickness and eating more.

Maddy broke and beat together four eggs. She figured Sandy could eat two and Zach could eat two. She decided to toast five pieces of bread. Zach might eat three. With butter and homemade fig jam, that should satisfy him. Shouldn't it?

As she was debating whether to add a fifth egg to the mixture, just in case, Sandy came into the kitchen. She went to the refrigerator and poured herself a glass of purple juice from a carton of tropical fruit punch. It was the only juice that didn't make her sick.

"Morning," Maddy said. "How're you feeling?"

Sandy sat down at the table and drank a few sips. "Okay," she said. "Something smells good."

"That's just butter heating in the pan." *Five eggs*, Maddy decided. "You sound like you feel better. I don't think you've thought anything smelled good since I've been here." She beat the eggs a few more times with her fork then poured them into the hot pan and began moving them around slowly with a spatula as they solidified.

"I'm okay, I guess," Sandy murmured and took another sip of purple juice.

Zach pocketed his phone as he came in,

breathing in the smell of eggs and butter. Sandy smiled at him wanly, then lifted the purple liquid to her lips. She was freshly showered and dressed in a white sundress that fell loosely over her baby bump. She looked cool and pretty, if a little pale. "How're you feeling?" he asked her.

"I'm okay—" Sandy started, then she stopped. "No, I'm not! I don't want to leave!" Sandy said, slamming the glass down on the wooden table.

Maddy jumped.

"This is my home. It's— It was Tristan's home. Our friends are here. Our whole life is here. I don't want to go away." She was on the verge of tears, and the eggs and toast were growing cold on the plate in front of her. "Besides, what if—" She stopped, and tears started spilling out of her eyes and down her cheeks.

Zach stared down at his feet. He'd always had trouble being around a woman who was crying, mostly because he had no earthly idea what to do. His instinctive reaction was to fix it, any way he could, but he'd found out from long experience with his mother and several girlfriends that when the tears started, 99 percent of the time, no one could fix it. His usual reaction to a crying woman was to duck out of the room and wait. But he couldn't do that with Sandy.

First of all, he'd held her while she'd cried the night before. It would be rude and insensitive to run away this morning. Second, he was the one who had made her cry, and third, no matter how long it took for her to realize that she had no choice in the matter, he had to stand here and be the bad guy.

He knew what she'd almost said. *What if Tristan comes back?* He'd hoped that their talk last night would make her realize that whether the two strange men were real or not, her vision of Tristan had been a dream. But he supposed it was much too difficult for her to totally believe that yet, especially since Tristan's body hadn't been found.

But no matter how much she cried and protested, Zach was determined to get her away from Bonne Chance. He was not going to let anyone harm Sandy or her baby.

She would go to Baton Rouge with her mother-in-law, no matter how much she objected.

"But I don't want to be here, either," Sandy continued. "Those same people I love and want to live near won't leave me alone for five minutes to try to figure out how I'm going to do this without...Tris—" She sobbed, picked up the glass and slammed it down again. A little purple liquid sloshed out onto the wooden table.

"Sandy, listen to me," Maddy said, sitting down opposite her. "You've got to go. It's for your own safety and for your baby. You said you saw those men at your window. Think about what they could have done if they'd gotten inside."

"I *said*?" she repeated. "I *said* I saw them? What does that mean?" Sandy cried. "You don't believe me?" She looked from Maddy to Zach and back to Maddy. "Are you saying you think I dreamed it? Oh, my God, you think I dreamed the two men." She turned to Zach. "I know you think I dreamed that I saw Tristan and I do understand the things you told me last night. But please at least tell me that you don't think I'm crazy."

"Sandy, of course not," Maddy said. "Of course we don't think you're crazy. But the trouble is, we can't find any evidence that anyone was outside your window. We can't locate footprints in the long grass or find fingerprints anywhere. That certainly doesn't mean that the men weren't there. In fact, it means if they were there, then they're very good at covering their tracks. And *that* means you're not safe here."

"But you're sneaking me out of town. How are you going to make this work? Maddy, you're going to pretend to be me? You won't fool anyone. And you won't be able to keep them all quiet, either."

Zach looked up. "Sandy, don't worry about

how we're going to do it. I need you to go to Baton Rouge with Mrs. DuChaud. I've got a twenty-four-hour guard from a private agency to make sure you're safe."

"A guard?" The tears gathering in her eyes began to roll down her cheeks. She swiped them away with the back of her hand. "Does Mrs. DuChaud know about this? She's not going to like having a guard on her house. I don't know why you're insisting that I can't take care of myself. When have you ever known me not to be capable of handling anything that came along?"

"Sandy, listen to me," Zach said. "I *know* you can take care of yourself normally. But you're pregnant and you're shocked and exhausted and grieving. This is not the time for you to be taking up the charge. You need to let Maddy and me worry about who's been sneaking around the house."

But Sandy pushed the chair back from the table and jumped to her feet. She rounded the table in two seconds flat and was in Zach's face. "Listen to me, Zach Winter. I know you think you're such a spectacular undercover agent, sweeping in here and *saving the day*, and you think I should just hop to do what you want me to. Well, do you know what the words *undercover agent* mean to me?"

She took a shaky breath. "They mean an

empty casket being lowered into the ground, and crouching beside it, my husband's sad, heartbroken best friend, who's got this false *superhero* mask on whenever he thinks I'm looking at him. I have *always* fought my own battles, Zach. I want to fight this one *so bad*!" She doubled her fists and punched the air. "So bad that I can't even describe it."

He opened his mouth to speak, but Sandy wasn't finished and she talked right over him. "But I can't. As much as you want to keep me safe, I know that I have to keep him safe," she muttered, looking down and cupping her hands around her small bump. "So I have to trust you." She turned toward Maddy. "And you."

Maddy looked surprised. Sandy gave her a quick, sad smile. "Zach told me last night. He told me about his job and yours. I wish you had told me." She turned back to Zach. "I'll go, Zach. Promise me you'll make sure that Tristan didn't—didn't die in vain."

AROUND NOON THAT DAY, Mrs. DuChaud drove out of Bonne Chance and headed home to Baton Rouge. Sandy had agreed to lie down on the backseat with a light blanket over her until they were at least an hour out of Bonne Chance.

At the same time, Maddy packed empty suitcases in her rental car and drove it twenty-three miles to the next town, where she paid in advance for a week's parking in an enclosed garage. Then she waited at a coffee shop for Zach to come and pick her up and sneak her back into Tristan and Sandy's house.

Alone in the house after the two women had gone, Zach took a shower then headed downtown. He had about an hour before he needed to drive to Houma to pick up Maddy and sneak her back into Tristan's house under cover of darkness.

His first stop was at the doctor's office. The sign on the door read James Trahill, MD. Zach opened the door and found himself facing an old wooden desk with a middle-aged, wooden-faced woman sitting behind it.

"May I help you?" she asked without changing expression.

"I'd like to see the doctor," Zach said with exaggerated patience.

The woman glanced up at him over her reading glasses. "Problem?" she asked.

"I just need to talk to him."

"Name?"

"Zachary Winter." He waited. He didn't recognize the woman, but he figured she was about the same age as his mother, or maybe a little older, so she might know his name.

"Winter," she whispered as she picked the

letters out laboriously on the keyboard in front of her. She painstakingly went through the dozens of questions needed by Dr. Trahill. By the time she'd finished, Zach felt as though he'd prefer Chinese water torture to her painfully slow typing.

Then she looked up at him with that wooden expression and asked again, "Problem?"

"Extreme anxiety," Zach said through clenched teeth. "Now."

The woman nodded and typed the two words, spelling them out in a whisper as she pecked. "Have a seat," she said.

Zach eyed the door behind her left shoulder. "Is he with someone?" he asked.

"No," she answered, still looking at the keyboard. Then she looked up at him, but she was too late. "No, wait. He's—"

Zach had already sidestepped her desk. He opened the door behind her. There were three doors in the hall. One was open. Zach looked in and saw a man in his forties with a receding hairline reading a chart through large glasses.

"Dr. Trahill?" Zach said.

"What?" The man looked up. "Yes?" He glanced at an appointment calendar then back at Zach. "Do you have an appointment?"

Zach shook his head. "No." He told him his

name and whom he worked for and quickly explained what he needed.

"I'm not sure—" Dr. Trahill started.

"Look," Zach snapped, propping his fists on the desk and bending over the doctor. "I can have my superior call you and explain the importance of cooperating with me. It won't take long. A couple of hours, and he'll want you to read and initial a few forms. What I need is very simple. Just some advice. I want to make people think a pregnant woman is sick, sick enough to be in bed and, if possible, it should be dangerous for her to have any visitors, but wouldn't require hospitalization."

Dr. Trahill frowned. "What's this about? It sounds suspicious—"

"Did you hear what I told you? I work for the National Security Agency. The agency and I need you to work with us on this, Doctor. I'm sure you want to help your country, right?"

Trahill's lips compressed as he tapped the tip of a ballpoint pen on his desk blotter. After a few seconds, his gaze met Zach's. "This is a little thin, but she could have a virus that compromises her immune system."

Zach liked the sound of that. "Compromises her immune system. You mean, she could catch something from her visitors."

The doctor nodded. "Very easily."

"That would be guaranteed to keep people away from her? They'd be afraid of infecting her and hurting the baby?"

Dr. Trahill nodded. "But if she truly were immuno-compromised, I would have her transported to the hospital in Houma and placed in isolation, for her safety and her baby's."

Zach drew in a sharp impatient breath. "I get that, Doc. But I can't do this in a hospital in the next town. I need her here, in her own home. Now, my bet is that you can tell your receptionist out there about Sandy DuChaud's compromised immune system, and within less than an hour, the word will be spread all over town. Am I right?"

The look on the doctor's face told Zach that he was on target. The receptionist probably had a network better than Twitter for getting information out to her friends and neighbors.

"I still don't like this," Trahill complained. "What's this all about and what does the NSA have to do with it?"

Zach got in the doctor's face again. "Trust me, Doc. The less you know about this, the safer you and your family and, in fact, the entire town will be. All I can tell you is that this is a matter of *national security*. Do you understand that?"

Trahill nodded nervously.

"And if *that* gets out, Doctor, you will be tried for treason. Do you understand *that*?"

His eyes behind his big glasses grew impossibly wide, but he nodded. His Adam's apple bobbed as he swallowed. "I swear," he whispered, raising his right hand. "I swear, as God is my witness—"

Zach growled and turned on his heel. At the door, he turned back, figuring a little extra insurance wouldn't hurt. "Oh, by the way, we've got all your phones and hers—" he nodded toward the waiting room "—bugged. Not to mention many other phones in town. Remember, the only thing that needs to be talked about in town is that Sandy is sick and she can't have any visitors. Got that, Dr. Trahill? Because the NSA is listening to everything you say."

Zach left, tipping an imaginary hat to the receptionist as he passed her desk. He wondered if his assessment of the doctor as a timid man who was a closet conspiracy theorist was correct. It was a gamble. If he was a conspiracy nut, he'd be eating up all the intrigue and secrecy, savoring all of Zach's warnings until the danger was over and he could act the hero for being part of the secret mission. If he wasn't a nut, well—maybe he was a staunch patriot and would keep quiet anyhow.

Either way, it was done now. Within an hour,

the whole town would be talking about *poor Sandy*, who was sick and quarantined in her own home, with her dead husband's best friend taking care of her. Each and every neighbor and friend would be trying to figure out ways to get a glimpse of her or give her a get-well card or just *speak to her for one second, to let her know we're all thinking about her.*

Zach liked the idea the doctor had given him of a reason to keep her quarantined. A compromised immune system. It meant that Sandy would be susceptible to all kinds of infections, as would her baby. It was a serious complication without any visible symptoms. So if anyone did catch a glimpse of Maddy masquerading as Sandy, there would be no clue that she really wasn't ill.

Chapter Seven

By the time Zach picked up Maddy in Houma and drove back to Tristan's house, it was dark. There was no enclosed garage, but Zach pulled into the driveway as close to the patio as he could get, so he could hurry Maddy inside with as little exposure as possible.

"Do you have the hair color and the blouses?" Zach asked her as she got out of the passenger side of the car.

"Yes, Zach. Right here. Just like when you asked me at the coffee shop. I'll color my hair tonight and wear one of these lovely oversize tops tomorrow. Is it okay if I don't wear maternity jeans?"

"What?" he asked, not quite sure what she'd said. Something about jeans. "Sure," he answered absently as he surveyed the front and side yards, making sure there was no one around. Tristan's house was eight miles from town and about a mile from a narrow, finger-like bayou on the Gulf, at the end of a long, dead-end driveway, and he'd seen no cars out this way, but he still wanted to be 100 percent sure that he wasn't placing Maddy in any unnecessary danger.

He'd thought about standing guard through the night in case the men Sandy had seen at the window came back. His instinct was to take over and do lookout and guard duty himself every night and let Maddy sleep safely inside. But he knew that wasn't practical or smart. They needed to share duties so one of them didn't get too tired to be effective. After all, they were both specially trained undercover agents, capable of performing the same duties.

He didn't want anyone to see Maddy, and he sure didn't want to expose her to danger, but on the other hand, he hadn't slept at all the night before. If he didn't sleep tonight, he'd be worthless by morning.

Just as Maddy unlocked the French doors and went inside, Zach saw a flash of light from the back of the house.

"Maddy!" he cried softly.

She stopped and turned.

"Get into Sandy's bedroom now!" he whispered.

"What's wrong?"

"Saw something. Get in there in case they try

to get in!" he commanded, drawing his weapon and pulling a high-powered flashlight from a small strap on his holster. "Shoot if you have to!" he added as she closed the French doors.

Zach moved toward the side edge of the house. He pressed his back against the wall and sidled along it until he reached the back corner. By then he could hear someone—or something— sneaking through the overgrown lawn. Carefully, he rolled sideways enough that he could get a glimpse around the corner.

A dark shadow, barely darker than the tangled jungle of vines and trees, was moving through the grass toward the swamp in a half crouch that left the upper third of its body exposed. The sky was cloudy enough to obscure the moon and a fine mist hung in the air. Still, Zach could tell that the shadow was human, but all he could see was a silhouette, so he couldn't tell if the person was a man or woman or if they were carrying a weapon.

All at once, Maddy was behind him. How he knew it was her, he wasn't sure, but when he half turned, there she was. "What is it?" he whispered.

"Someone's been in Sandy's room. It's a mess."

Zach cursed under his breath just as he heard

more rustling movement out in front of him. "Get back inside," he commanded Maddy.

"Not on your life," she whispered harshly. "I'm sticking with you. You have no idea how many of them are out there."

"Damn it, Maddy—" he started, but a glint of light stopped him. "Did you see that?" he whispered.

"That flash of light? Was it a gun?"

"Maybe." He raised his weapon and aimed in that direction. "I'm a law enforcement agent and I'm armed! Stop! Stop right now or I'll shoot."

He heard the rustle of leaves and branches and the crunch of twigs and shells as the person picked up speed, headed toward the water. "Stop now! Stop or I'll shoot!" he cried, but the person kept running.

So he aimed carefully and shot a round that landed about three feet in front of the running shadow.

The person jumped and made a startled sound, then froze in place. Zach was ready. He aimed his flashlight directly at the head and turned it on. The intense beam lit a dark, narrow face with eyes that gleamed like small fires. Another startled sound, this one a deep grunt, echoed through the darkness. It sounded like a man.

"Stop! Right now!" Zach yelled, but the face

disappeared from the flashlight's beam and the sound of feet and legs moving through underbrush got louder. "You out there. I *will* shoot again. Stop!"

Then Zach saw a flash and heard a blast. He grabbed Maddy and threw her and himself to the ground, all in one split second. He landed right on top of her a fraction of a second after he heard her almost silent *"Oof."*

The crunch of leaves and twigs hit his ears as the man sprinted through the tangled canopy of cypress and mangrove trees and oleander bushes that made up the overgrown swampland in south Louisiana.

Zach got his legs under him and started to rise, freeing his gun hand to take a shot if necessary, but his ears were buzzing and something warm tickled his right ear. Keeping his gun hand ready, he reached with his left hand to brush at his ear. His fingers came away wet and sticky. *Son of a bitch.* He'd been shot.

"Zach! You're bleeding."

Maddy's wide blue eyes stared up at him in horror. She reached up to touch his ear, but he avoided her hand and rolled off her. He'd instinctively held himself above her on his elbows and knees, but even so, the position was suggestive and uncomfortable. For him, it had gotten extremely uncomfortable, and he hadn't even been aware of his position or the sensations that had been aroused until he'd already rolled off her.

It showed that there were certain responses of the body that didn't require a conscious decision by the brain. Because if he'd had a chance to make a conscious decision, he'd have vetoed that particular position before he'd gotten himself into it.

Even as those thoughts flitted through his brain, he'd rolled up to his knees and was searching the dark perimeter of the yard for any indication of the man—or men—who'd broken into the house and shot at them.

Maddy flipped over onto her stomach and scooted around him, placing herself behind him again. He nodded. She'd done the right thing. She was armed, but he was tacitly in charge, and she had taken the secondary position without question or argument.

MADDY GRIPPED HER SIG as if it was her only lifeline. Seeing Zach bleeding had shaken her. The wound was just above his temple, and blood was spilling down the side of his face and trickling into his ear. She squeezed the handle of the gun more tightly, hoping her death grip would stop her hands from shaking. It helped a little.

She knew he wasn't badly hurt or he wouldn't be able to move as smoothly and freely as he did. But she also knew from first and second aid, that wounds, particularly head wounds, could exhibit delayed reactions. And she was sure he wouldn't allow her to look at his injury until the threat was gone.

So she stayed where she was and suppressed the urge to wipe the blood off his temple. He inched forward, holding his weapon pointed at the last place where he'd heard a sound. His left hand supported his right and he held the high-powered flashlight in the supporting hand, ready to flip on at a split second's notice.

He'd grown perfectly still and had angled his head to listen. She tuned her instincts as close to his as she possibly could. She drew herself up and tensed her muscles, ready for anything. Her blood burned and surged in her veins and her hyperfocused brain intensified and slowed every sound, every separate movement, as if the rest of the world was moving in super slow motion, and she and Zach were the only ones still in normal time.

To her, it sounded as if the person or people were running away. The sounds were fading. She glanced at Zach again. He angled his head so slightly she could have missed it, but she didn't. A thrill erupted deep inside her. He was thinking the same thing. It was a small thing, but she felt their connection.

They were in perfect sync, so attuned to each other that they might be one person. It was an exciting and extraordinarily intimate feeling. Yet nothing about it, not even the thrill that had arrowed through her, was distracting. In fact, it was a powerful and energizing sensation.

Zach turned his head and met her gaze. For an instant, they stood perfectly still. Then, as if they had a private, telepathic code, the two of them relaxed at the same time.

"Gone," Zach whispered.

Maddy took a step backward and Zach did the same. They moved back to the patio doors and slipped inside, still in sync, their shoulders barely touching. As soon as they were inside, they stood shoulder to shoulder, listening, watching, feeling. The house was empty; Maddy felt rather than heard or saw Zach nod.

"Clear," Zach said, lowering his weapon.

"Clear," Maddy agreed as she relaxed her right hand. It cramped and ached, she'd been holding the gun so tightly.

Still under the influence of their connection, Maddy turned toward him just as he turned toward her. Her eyes had adapted to the dark, and the lights from the oil platforms out on the water, combined with the lights from the town of Bonne Chance north of them, lent enough of a pale glow that she could make out Zach's form, if not his features, in front of her.

She took a deep, shaky breath.

"What was that?" Zach asked in a whisper.

"The intruders?" Maddy said, knowing full well they weren't what he was talking about, but here in the aftermath of their coordinated effort to protect the house and each other, she was shy about saying anything. If Zach let it drop, then she would, too.

"No," he said, shaking his head. "You know what I'm talking about."

"Yes," she whispered.

He took a step toward her, which put them toe to toe. His eyes glimmered with the pale lights from the south and the north. He was staring at her so intently that another thrill, a different kind of thrill, surged through her and settled deep, deep inside her.

He brought his hand up to touch her cheek, and the cold, jellylike texture of congealing blood from his fingers startled her until she remembered that he'd been shot.

"I need to clean that," she said, "and make certain you're okay. I'm sure there's some antiseptic around here somewhere," she said, but he pressed his thumb against her lips, stopping her words. "Not yet," he said softly, handing her a handkerchief from his pocket. "Just wipe it clean. It's only a graze. It's stopped bleeding already."

As she brushed the handkerchief across his skin, he kissed her. At first, his mouth was soft, his kiss slow and tentative. Maddy loved the feel of his mouth, which could look so hard, soft against her lips. But she wondered if she'd been wrong about him, about his need to be in charge. Was he really going to kiss her as if she were some fragile Southern belle? If so, she was not going to be happy.

He lifted his head to look into her eyes, his dancing with emerald green light, then he kissed her again, and this time there was nothing slow or soft about it. His mouth was hard, as she'd expected it to be. Hard and sensual on hers, demanding. He tasted her lips and she parted them so he could delve inside, deepening the kiss, until she was breathless.

The flame that had ignited in her the first moment she'd seen him flared. She gave him back his kisses, filled with as much yearning, as much need, as he'd shown her.

Then he changed the game again. Now he nibbled softly on her lips, her cheeks, the lobes of her ears, wispy tender nibbles that made her crazy with the need for more. Just when she thought she couldn't stand another ticklish brush of his lips against her nose and cheek, he grabbed her jaw between his fingers and thumb and ravished her mouth with hot, hard kisses that thrust and retreated, thrust and retreated, like the act of sex.

She gave as good as she got, kissing him back, grazing his tongue and lips with her teeth, darting her tongue in and out until his breaths rasped harshly in his throat.

"What is this?" he asked in a labored whisper.

Maddy drew back enough to free her mouth to speak. She didn't have to ask him what he was talking about, because she knew. They were still in sync. Still reacting in perfect tune.

"I don't know," she murmured. "Something happened out there. Something clicked. We were perfect. Connected somehow, so that together, we were better than the two of us alone. We were—" she laughed shyly "—like a supersoldier."

"I still feel it," he said, pulling her close and holding her tightly, pressing his lips against her hair.

"I know. Me, too." She lifted her head and kissed him again. "It's like we know each other's moves. Almost know each other's thoughts."

Zach's chest rumbled with a low laugh. "Do you know what I'm thinking right now?" he asked.

"Yes, I do," she said with a soft smile. "And

I think it's a wonderful idea." As soon as she said it, she felt him shut down, as if he'd flipped a switch.

"I'm not so sure."

Maddy winced. "What?"

"There were intruders in the house. We need to see what they took."

"Now?" she said. "Really? They're gone. Don't break the spell. I'm so ready for you my legs are weak. Please don't stop now." She kissed him again and again, then helped him remove his shirt and began nipping at his lips, his chin, then down to his collarbone and the firm planes of his pecs and breastbone. Then she turned to his nipples, those tiny erect nubs that made her mouth water just looking at them.

When she licked one of them, Zach groaned and grabbed her upper arms, trying to push her away.

"Hey," she said, trying to keep it light. "Don't push me away. These are two of my favorite things. And they're delicious." She grazed her teeth along the sensitized tip of the nipple. He arched and thrust his arousal against her.

"Oh, yes," she gasped. "That's it."

He thrust again, the hard length of him rubbing insistently against her.

"Zach, please," she begged. "Don't stop."

"Not sure I can now," he muttered, pressing even harder.

Maddy reached around him and caught his buttocks and pulled him to her. He rocked back and forth, his arousal rubbing against her, driving her crazy.

"Zach!" she cried, feeling the exquisite ache that foretold orgasm. "Please, too much. Wait."

But he didn't wait. He pulled her close and continued to rock against her rhythmically until her body succumbed to his exquisite pressure. Her world exploded in a climax that caused spots before her eyes. She cried out and collapsed against him, until his arms embracing her were the only things keeping her from falling.

"Oh," she exhaled. "Oh."

He pressed his cheek against hers and nibbled on her earlobe.

"Are you—" she started, but a shake of his head stopped her.

"Don't worry about me," he said. "That was for you."

At last, she felt as though she could put weight on her legs without them collapsing. She stood shakily, but she didn't pull away from his kisses and caresses. "Do you still think this is not a good idea?" she asked him, touching his nose with the tip of her finger.

He met her gaze and nodded. "Actually…"

She covered his mouth with hers. "Don't say it," she mumbled with her lips pressed against his, then she kissed him earnestly, took his hand and led him into the nursery. She pushed him down onto the couch and climbed on top of him. When she started unzipping his pants, he groaned, but he didn't stop her. Within seconds, their clothes were gone and she was showering his face, neck and pecs with kisses.

When he lifted her above him and pushed into her, she nearly cried in exquisite pleasure. But just as she feared a tear was going to escape her eye, he turned them both over together and began to make love to her until she reached heights of pleasure she'd never experienced before. That night she came more times than she ever had in her life.

As their passion waned and they settled into the afterglow, Maddy discovered that she felt even more like crying than she had earlier. She'd never liked crying. It was a waste of time and made her nose and eyes red. So she held her breath and refused to let even one tear fall.

She didn't know what she would say if Zach asked her what was wrong. She didn't want to tell him that making love with him was the sweetest thing she'd ever known, and she was sure it was because of the connection they'd discovered. What if he had no idea what she was talking

about? What if the only time he felt their connection was when they were facing danger.
What if for him, sex with her was a pastime, a
fill-in because there were no elegant supermodel
types in Bonne Chance? She lay there, afraid
he'd notice her tears, but when several minutes
passed and he didn't say anything, she lifted her
head and saw that he'd fallen asleep.

Chapter Eight

Maddy woke early the next morning. She was lying close—very close—to Zach. Practically on top of him, in fact. His long, leanly muscled body was pressed against the front of her, and the back of the sofa was tight against her back. She tried to suppress a giggle. She was caught between the devil and the deep blue sofa. *Ha-ha-ha.*

Zach shifted and Maddy closed her eyes as aftershocks of the multiple orgasms he'd given her rippled through her body. His runner's muscles, normally rock hard, were still firm, but at the same time supple and loose. But even as she noticed, he tensed and they went rock hard again. And that wasn't all that was rock hard.

But Maddy's bravado from the night before had turned to shyness in the light of day. With a push, she sprang up and away from him. Or at least she tried to. Just as she pushed, his arm tightened around her.

"Whoa! Ow!" His eyes popped open and a pained expression contorted his face. "Hey!"

"Sorry," she said as she wriggled away and scrambled over to the far arm of the sofa, relieved to see that at some point during the night she'd managed to put her pajamas on. He drew in a harsh breath through his teeth. "Yeah," he said. "Watch your knees. You could really hurt someone."

"Sorry," she said again. "I was a little surprised when I woke up there." She waved her hand toward him and the sofa.

"Are you saying you don't remember last night?"

"I remember last night," she said, her face beginning to flush. "What I don't remember is going to sleep, and I certainly don't remember putting my pajamas on."

"You remember taking them off?" he asked, his mouth quirked in a half smile.

She chuckled. "I remember somebody did."

"I remember lying next to you afterward. You snuggled right into my side. Next thing I know, it's light out and you're kicking me in the—"

"Okay," she said quickly, interrupting him. "Got it." She stood and stretched, yawning. "Oh, I'm stiff."

Zach grunted as he pushed himself up off the sofa. "Yeah," he said wryly. "Me, too."

Maddy's face heated up again, so she hurried out of the room and across the hall into the master bedroom. A half hour later, when she emerged from Sandy's bedroom, having showered in the master bath, she nearly bumped into Zach, who had just stepped out of the hall bath, a towel precariously tied at his waist and his hair wet and spiky. He looked incredibly handsome, with his golden skin shining with water droplets. His eyes were brilliant green and highlighted by his long, wet lashes.

He smiled. "Sorry," he said. "I thought I'd beat you out of the shower by at least a half hour."

"I do a pretty fast shower," she said, pulling her terry-cloth robe more tightly around her. She scooted around him and into the guest bedroom.

"Hey," Zach called after her.

She turned to look at him and regretted it. The towel had slipped and appeared ready to fall any second. She focused on the corner of the ceiling. "What is it?"

"As soon as we have breakfast, I want to walk down to the water and take a look around. It's rained a good bit, but I'm hoping I can find evidence that someone has used the DuChauds' old boat dock recently. Maybe I can pick up some tracks or shoe prints. If nothing else, I can talk to one or two of the old fishermen who still go down there to fish."

"I'll go with you," she said.

"No, you won't. You're supposed to be pregnant and in bed, under quarantine. You're not leaving the house."

She pressed her lips together and shot him a look that would have worked better if she'd had real lasers behind it. "You really want me lying around in bed? That's your plan? I thought it was just a cover story for the doctor to tell the folks in town. I'm not going to stay in bed."

"How about a compromise? You don't have to stay in bed, just in the bedroom and straighten up the mess the intruders left. Maybe you can figure out what they were looking for."

She rolled her eyes. "I guess I walked into that one, didn't I? What about the sheriff? We didn't call last night. Should I call now to report the B and E?"

Zach shot her a look. "What do you think?" he said.

She evaluated his expression. "So I'm thinking no. I'll straighten everything up and see if I can find anything there. Don't worry about me. I don't mind cleaning up."

"Listen to me," he continued. "Here's something else you can do. I want you to contact the captain of the oil rig again and tell him you're really being pressured to make that *spot inspection*. Was that what you called it?"

Maddy held the robe tight at her neck and wished that Zach would put a hand on the towel that was doing a really poor job of staying up. She was sure it had slipped another inch. She averted her gaze.

"That's a complete waste of time," she said to the wall. "He's not going to let an inspector on his rig now. And he's got the perfect excuse. All he has to say is that he's in the middle of an investigation into the death of one of his employees and he's home free. Nobody would complain and nobody will force him to let me on there."

"We could sneak aboard, couldn't we?"

Maddy forgot that she wasn't supposed to be looking at him. She fixed him with a stare. "Sneak aboard? No. There are security cameras everywhere, and the communications officer and the security chief monitor them. They'd probably shoot us first and ask questions later."

Zach shrugged and the towel began to slip. He caught it and gave her a sheepish grin. "Talk to you in a minute," he said.

IT WAS AFTER NOON before Zach could get in touch with Dr. Trahill. After finally reaching him at home during Sunday dinner after church, he and Trahill met in the doctor's office. Zach wanted to look him in the eye and assure himself that Trahill still understood the importance of their secret plan to national security and the consequence of revealing it to anyone.

Then he checked in with the medical examiner to see if he had any more information regarding Tristan's remains.

Dr. Bookman told Zach that the Coast Guard was calling off the search as of that morning. "But I do have stomach contents of two sharks that I'm sending off for DNA matching."

Zach swallowed hard, feeling a little queasy at the ME's words. "Will you call Mrs. DuChaud and let her know about the search?" he asked. "I'd really appreciate it." The ME agreed.

So it was noon by the time Zach got down to the small dock that Tristan's grandfather had built to tie up his fishing boat and his pirogue. As Zach approached the dock, the ground got muddier. At least he'd had the foresight to grab Tristan's rubber knee-high boots and binoculars as he'd left the house. The gumbo mud was already sucking at the boots. Wet from the rain, it was as greedy as quicksand.

Taking what appeared to be the driest path, Zach stepped onto the first creaky boards of the dock. He stood there for a short while, gazing out over the Gulf, orienting himself not only in space but also in time. It had been thirteen years since he'd stood here with Tristan and fantasized about setting out to sea to become pirates or privateers or stowaways on a ship headed for a faraway land.

A deep sadness, mixed with a poignant sense of loss, enveloped him as he looked out on the same waters, the same sky and maybe even the same trees as they'd gazed at all those years ago.

"Ah, Tristan," he muttered. "You were always such a freaking hero. Why'd you have to go and get killed for? I always thought I'd come back, man." He shook his head. "I'm sorry, Tris. I'm sorry I wasn't here to help you."

After a long time, Zach rubbed his eyes and surveyed the water that was brown near the shore but began to reflect the blue of the sky that stretched out to meet it at a distant horizon he couldn't even distinguish. To him it looked as if the whole round world was spread out before him. A beautiful, treacherous world that could steal friends, enemies and loved ones as easily as it could yield up nourishing food to a hungry world.

Then, as he shaded his eyes from the sun, he thought he saw a tiny dark dot way out on the water. He used the binoculars to try to see it closer. When he finally zeroed in on the dot, he saw that it was a cruise ship, either coming into or leaving the Port of New Orleans.

For a moment, he'd thought it might be the *Pleiades Seagull*. He'd learned it was one of the closest rigs, probably no more than twenty to twenty-five miles out from shore. Of course, the horizon didn't stretch that far.

Maddy had told him that the *Seagull* was located on top of a deep canyon on the floor of the Gulf, much deeper than one might expect so close to shore.

A pang of something pricked him in the chest. He wasn't sure what the feeling was. Excitement, anxiety or more grief. He lowered the binoculars and pressed his knuckles into the middle of his chest, where the ache had settled.

"Hey, you!" a voice called out. "Whacha doing here, you?"

Zach whirled. For an instant his mind made the voice Tristan's. He'd often affected the strong Cajun accent of his grandfather and father.

"Hold on!" the man shouted. "You stay, you!"

Zach froze because the man he saw standing at the edge of the cypress swamp was holding a big shotgun. A 12 gauge. It was an old gun that cocked by hand. As he watched, not breathing, the man cocked the right barrel, then the left, and aimed them both right at him.

Something familiar about the man played at the edge of Zach's mind as he held his hands up, palms out. He'd probably met him before, back when he and Tristan explored the overgrown paths and hiding places in the swamp. But he couldn't be sure. It had been a long time, and to his recollection, Woodrow, or Boudreau or whatever his name was, had been old back then.

"Boudreau?" he said, his tongue sliding over the *B* in a way that could have been interpreted as either name. "Is that you?"

The man's chin lifted and he eyed Zach with eyes as black and fiery as coals on fire. "Who that?" he said.

"I'm Zach Winter. I was a friend of Tristan's." Zach didn't move, but he nodded in the direction of Tristan's house.

The man's eyes seemed to glow with more fire. "Tristán?" He used the French pronunciation with the accent on the second syllable. "Who you to know young Tristán? He ain't here no more, him. You know what happen to Tristán, you? Or you just here to try an' trick me?"

Zach noticed that the old man's mouth only moved on one side when he talked, and now he also noticed that his left eye was a little more squinty than the right. Also that his left hand, which was holding the gun by the stock, was trembling. Had he had a stroke? He decided he didn't want to give the man any information that he didn't already have, so he answered his questions with a question.

Shaking his head, he said, "I'm not here to trick you. Don't you know what happened?"

Boudreau stared at Zach for a long time. It was beginning to feel uncomfortably long by the time he spoke. "You the *chef menteur*, you. The chief liar round these parts. I might be a little tetch'd in the head, but I ain't that bad. I know *le diable* when I meet him." He held up a hand to cover his eyes. "I can't look at you, no. Can't look at the devil."

"Boudreau, I'm not the devil. I'm Tristan's friend, from school," Zach said.

"You no friend of Tristán, you. No sirree. You a devil." He lifted the shotgun, his left hand trembling more.

"Okay, okay, Boudreau—" Zach started.

"Don't call me that, you hear?" the old man said. "You call me M'sieu Boudreau, you."

"Monsieur Boudreau, have you seen any folks back in here that shouldn't be here? Maybe coming from one of the oil rigs or from another town?"

"Oil rigs? Is that where you from? You *are* the devil, then. They need to be burned, those nasty things. They make the water poison." Boudreau nodded. He kept nodding until Zach thought maybe he'd drifted off to sleep with his eyes open. The shotgun's barrel drooped a little, a little more and a little more.

Zach took a tentative step toward his car.

Boudreau's head stopped nodding and the barrel of the gun raised. "Whoa there, you," he said. "I ain't exactly decided what to do with you."

"Monsieur Boudreau," Zach said respectfully. "I wondered if you'd seen anybody around here who wasn't supposed to be here. Anybody who disturbed you or woke you at night or anything."

For an instant Boudreau's eyes lost their fire and went opaque. "Nah sirree," he said. "There been some sneaky bastards in the woods, but they don't come near me, them. Nah sirree. I guarantee they know better than that. Yeah." The fire reignited. "Now, you, you go on and get out of here. You got no business on DuChaud land, you. I don't know you. Nobody know you. You don't look like nobody I ever knew."

The old Cajun stood staunchly, holding the gun in his good right hand and his trembling left hand, and waited. When Zach didn't move immediately, Boudreau gestured with the barrel of the gun.

"Monsieur?" Zach tried one more time.

"Go on, you. Go on. Leave us alone down here. Folks gotta heal. Don't need nobody like you coming in and upsetting 'em."

Zach walked to his car, acutely aware of the shotgun pointed at his back.7

ON HIS WAY back to the house, Zach called the priest. "Duff?"

"Yes?" Duff said in a subtly disapproving voice. "Who is this? Zach? Is that you?"

"Yeah," Zach said. "I mean, yes, Father Michael."

"What can I do for you?"

"Is old Boudreau still around? The old man who used to live on Tristan's property way back when we were kids?"

There was a pause. "Actually, I don't know. I don't think I've heard anybody mention Boudreau in years. I'm not sure anybody's seen him around in all that time. How old would he be now?"

"I don't know," Zach said. "Tristan and I thought he was older than dirt back when we were about ten or eleven. But now that I think about it, he might not have been more than sixty or so. What do you think? When was the last time you saw him?"

"It's been a long, long time. Why?"

"I think it was Boudreau who ran me off Tristan's boat dock just a few minutes ago. He wouldn't tell me his name, but he had an old 12-gauge shotgun like I remember he used to carry. No dog, but then that old bluetick hound that followed him around was probably eight or nine years old back then."

"Boudreau ran you off Tristan's property? I declare I'd have said he was dead. What do you think he's been living on all this time? He never, and I mean seriously *never*, comes to town. If he ever gets coffee or sugar or even beans, I don't know where he gets 'em."

Zach pulled into the driveway and parked near the French doors. "I remember Tristan was always fascinated with him. He used to tell me that Boudreau ate dandelion and chicory greens and ground up the chicory root and roasted it to make coffee. Said he ate possum and gator and rabbit. And sometimes he might kill a wild pig. Tristan said he could smell it roasting and he'd go over there with potatoes and carrots and onions and eat with him."

"Over where?" Duff asked.

"I'm not sure. I followed Tristan into the swamp to Boudreau's stick house a few times, but I couldn't have gotten there by myself back then, much less now. Okay, well, thanks. I guess he's just old and kind of crazy now. I asked him a few questions, but he didn't make much sense."

"Well, I do recall him having a stroke a few years ago. Tristan took him to the doctor but he wouldn't go to the hospital. Zach, what are you doing snooping around here?"

"Just helping Sandy out. I'm helping her with Tristan's papers."

Duff was silent and Zach knew he didn't believe him. He took a breath to try and convince him that what he was telling him was true, but Duff spoke first.

"Don't get involved in this, whatever it is, Zach. Take some advice from someone who knows. All it'll do is engulf your every waking and sleeping thought."

Zach knew Duff wasn't talking about Tristan's death. He was talking about Fox Moncour's death years ago. "Don't worry, Duff. I'm fine. I can handle it."

Zach said goodbye and hung up, thinking about what Duff had said about Boudreau. Maybe Boudreau had suffered a stroke, but his eyes burned like fiery coals and his voice had been clear. Zach was still half-convinced that the Cajun was crazy. He was more than half-convinced that if Boudreau saw him again, he'd shoot him with that 12 gauge.

"Maddy?" he called out when he entered the house after taking off the rubber boots outside the door. "Is the alarm on?"

Maddy came out of Sandy's bedroom with her newly colored hair damp and waving around her face. She blew a strand out of her eye. "No. I didn't turn it on. It's been deathly quiet. I was wishing for an MP3 player or a TV."

"They don't have a TV?" Zach asked.

"Not in the bedroom."

"Oh. Find anything?"

"You mean, did I find anything *missing*? No. But then, it's kind of hard to find something missing. I did find a partial footprint right under the window."

"Inside the room? I looked. I didn't see a footprint."

Maddy smiled. "No, you didn't because it was mostly water with just a faint bit of mud to color it. It was almost totally dry. I went over the floor with a flashlight, looking for something like that. Of course, I couldn't pick it up because I don't have the equipment. It might have come from the kind of boots the guys wear on the platform, but even if we were able to make a plaster cast or even just lift the print onto some sticky paper, we're talking about over four hundred men. Not to mention the men in town— which would be what?—twice or three times that many or more."

Zach grimaced. "No fingerprints, either?"

"Again, I don't have the equipment. I've heard of using soot from a candle, a makeup brush and cellophane tape, but I've never tried it."

"Try it. I'm not ready to let the sheriff know anything about us smuggling Sandy out of town, but you could get Homeland Security to run the print, couldn't you? If your method works, we can photograph it and send it to your lab."

"We use the FBI, but yes. We can do that. I'll talk to my handler."

Chapter Nine

"Okay, then," Maddy said. "Um, thanks, Brock." She pressed the off key on her phone with a finger that felt numb. All her fingers felt numb. She sat on the bed, trying to go over in her head what Brock had just told her. But her brain felt as numb as her fingers. He'd warned her, but she hadn't really believed him, she supposed.

"Maddy?"

Zach's voice floated across the hall from the nursery, where he'd set up Sandy's laptop. He'd spent all morning trying to find something— anything—that would give them a clue about what had gotten Tristan killed and put Sandy's life in danger.

"Yeah?" she answered Zach without even trying to raise her voice enough that he could actually hear her.

"Maddy!" She heard chair legs scraping on the hardwood floors and, sure enough, within a second, there he was at the door. Unconsciously, she smiled when she saw him. It was such a pleasure just to look at him, to let her eyes rest on his handsome face or allow her gaze to travel over his lean masculine body.

"Come here for a minute, will you? I want to show you something."

She nodded. "Sure."

"Maddy?"

She looked up. "Mmm?"

"What's wrong?"

"What?" she asked. She hadn't really heard what he'd said. She was still a little stunned by what Brock had told her.

"You're still sitting there. Come look at Sandy's laptop."

She got up and followed him into the nursery. Her gaze went immediately to the shiny blue mobile Sandy had bought a couple of weeks ago to hang over the crib. She'd gotten it on the day the doctor had told her that although it was early, he was pretty confident that she was having a boy, based on what he'd seen on the ultrasound.

"Take a look at this. Does it mean anything to you?" Zach asked.

"What am I looking at?" she asked.

"This file name. It's a shortcut for an audio file."

"That one? Named SD? Have you listened to it?"

Zach shook his head. "The file's not on the computer. Just the shortcut. It was opened from removable media, like a flash drive."

"Is there a backup or a sampling somewhere on the hard drive or in memory?" Maddy asked.

"Not that I can find." Zach hit the arm of the computer chair with his fist. "Damn it."

"It's probably around here somewhere."

"I don't know," he said. "There are a million places Tristan could have hidden it. Anywhere in the house. In his car or Sandy's car. Somewhere in town. Hell, he could have hidden it somewhere on the rig."

"Do you think that's what the guys who broke in were looking for?"

"I don't know about that, either. Do they *know* that he recorded something? And even if they know that, do they know he put it on a flash drive? Or did somebody order them to search the house, just in case?"

Maddy sighed. "For that matter, how do we know the file is even Tristan's? SD probably stands for Sandy DuChaud. What if Sandy was making a recording of songs to play for the baby? Or recording herself doing karaoke? Or recording a daily journal for Tristan while he was offshore?"

Zach stood, sending the computer chair rolling back to slam against the side of the crib.

"You're right. We don't even know it's Tristan's. Hell, we don't know anything."

Maddy stood, too. "I know you're frustrated. I am, as well. I wish I knew something, but Sandy didn't mention anything about recording songs or a journal or anything to me. She never said anything to Tristan on the phone, either, if that's any consolation. So the flash drive is probably Tristan's."

"A lot of good that does us, since we have no clue where he might have hidden it. I made coffee if you want some." He stalked out.

Maddy wished she didn't have to tell him what Brock had told her, but she did, so she might as well get it over with. She followed him into the kitchen, where he was pouring a mug of coffee. She got some, too, with her usual three teaspoonfuls of sugar. She sat down at the kitchen table opposite him.

"Zach," she said once he'd had a couple of swallows. "I talked to my handler just a few minutes ago."

His gaze, which had been on the cup in his hand, met hers. "Yeah? Will he run the fingerprints for us?"

She took a sip of sweet, hot coffee. "I didn't get a chance to ask him. Zach, I'm being pulled off this case." Her voice cracked.

Zach's jaw worked, but that was the only sign

that what she'd said had even penetrated his consciousness. He took another swallow of coffee, then stood and tossed the rest into the sink and set the mug down on the counter. "Are they replacing you?" he asked flatly, as if all that mattered to him was that they send someone here to help him.

"Brock didn't say anything about that. All he said was that the director had decided that there was no more need for my services here." She took a breath. "I'm thinking no. They're not replacing me."

Zach went to the French doors and looked out, then looked at his watch. "I'm going to walk back down to the dock. I didn't get to look at everything earlier. I ran into an elderly Cajun man who's lived in the swamp near Tristan's house probably all his life." He reached for the doorknob.

"Zach, wait," she said. "I wanted to tell you that I'm not leaving. I'm taking vacation days, too, so I can stay here. I may not officially be on the case, but I can still help."

He turned around and looked at her, frowning. "What? Why?"

The question surprised her. "Why? Because I want to stay here. I want to help figure out what happened to Tristan."

"No."

The single word sparked her anger. She stood and walked around the table and stuck her forefinger into the middle of his chest. "I am Sandy's guest. You can't tell me no."

"I just did," he said calmly.

"You may have tried to, but you didn't, because you *can't*. I don't have to listen to you. I'm staying right here. Tristan's death is on my hands and I'm not walking away—"

Zach grabbed her wrist. "His death was not your fault. If it's anybody's fault, it's Homeland Security's for not getting him off that oil rig in time. You did your job and it sounds like you did it well. So stop blaming yourself and go home to New Orleans, where you're not in danger. I'll take care of this. It's not your problem."

"The hell it's not. You came barreling in here, bossing me around and getting in my way and making me—" She stopped. She couldn't say everything she wanted to say. She couldn't tell him how much she'd come to depend on him being there during the past three days. Or how safe she felt with him here.

"And making you what, Madeleine Tierney? And what? Getting in your way and what?"

She shook her head. "Nothing."

"Nothing?" he mocked. "Nothing?" He stepped closer and looked down at her. "Are you sure you weren't going to say something else? Like this?" He put his hand on her cheek, with his thumb beneath her chin, and lifted it, then bent his head and kissed her, gently at first, then harder and deeper. His fingers slid from her cheek around to the nape of her neck, and he held her there, kissing her until they were both breathless. Then he kissed her some more. He used his tongue like a weapon, thrusting and parrying and thrusting again until she was light-headed with excitement.

Zach wished he hadn't started this because he was pretty sure that nothing could stop him now, short of Maddy shooting him or at least coldcocking him. He loved to kiss her. So much that he thought he could spend the rest of his life doing that. Her beautiful turned-down mouth was the most sensual and delicious mouth he'd ever kissed. He pulled back for a moment to look at her and trace the shape of her lips with a finger. Then he bent and kissed her again.

She moaned deep in her throat, and he felt the low, sexy vibration all the way through him, down to his groin. He almost smiled. He liked keeping her off guard, keeping her enthralled, while holding himself in control until he could no longer stand it. He liked watching her as she became more and more turned on by him until she finally gave in to the pleasure he gave her.

He wanted to be the one who mastered the

situation, the dominant one. He wanted to kiss her senseless, knock her off her feet, make her world tilt. From the moment he'd realized that he wanted her, he'd longed to give her all the romantic clichés. Every one of them, from *opposites attract* to *happily-ever-after*, because he was sure that Madeleine Tierney didn't deal in clichés very often. She blazed her own trail and was and would always be the first one to take it.

She was an odd mix of fearlessness and vulnerability, and he had the feeling that he would never figure her out completely, not in fifty years or five hundred. He knew, though, that he'd be happy to spend all that time trying.

His own thoughts were turning him on to such an extent that he was having trouble controlling himself. Just as he was about to slow things down, Maddy turned the tables and took the aggressive role. She took his mouth in a passionate kiss that was as deep and intimate as any he had ever given or received. He pulled her to him, molding her body to his, amazed, just as he was the last time, at how well they fit together.

He was dying to rip his mouth away from hers and taste her cheek, her ear, her neck and that sexy little bump on her shoulder, the space between her breasts and the soft, firm globes themselves. But he knew he had to stop at least for a moment to get his breath, so he wouldn't embarrass himself.

When he pulled away, Maddy moaned again and crumpled handfuls of his shirt in her fists. "Don't stop," she said on a gasp. "What are you doing? Don't stop now."

But he held her there as he did his best to regain his breath. She was panting, too, her breath sawing in and out, in and out. "Ah," she said, frustrated, then looked up at him, pushing her hair out of her eyes.

He wrapped his arms around her and lifted her and set her on the kitchen table. Then he stepped between her legs and ran his palms up her thighs, across the rough material of her jeans. She wrapped her arms around his waist and pulled him closer, arching her back against his lower belly.

He bent and let his tongue trail down her neck to her collarbone and farther, tasting her between her breasts, one of the places he'd been dying to taste ever since he'd seen her in that little blue pajama top.

Spreading his hands, he wrapped his fingers around her ribs and placed his thumbs beneath her breasts, where he caressed the underside of them until she was panting. Then he pushed her shirt up and saw that she didn't have on a bra. With a soft gasp he lowered his head. His tongue and teeth found the nipple of her right breast beneath the thin cotton of the shirt. It sprang to erectness as he licked it and grazed it with his teeth.

"Oh," Maddy said. "Oh, please. Zach!"

He pulled back and blew on the nipple, feeling a thrill arrow through him when the tiny nub tightened and extended even more. Then he moved to the other breast and did the same. He'd known this was going to happen. He was on the edge. If he didn't slow down, at least long enough to get her jeans off, he was definitely going to embarrass himself in a big way.

He reached for the button on her jeans and, following his lead, she reached for the zipper and button on his pants.

Something banged against the door. Zach sprang away, whirled and drew his gun within a fraction of a second.

"What was that?" Maddy said.

Zach gulped in air as he scanned the patio through the paned windows. "I don't know," he said. "I don't see anything. Relaxing minutely, he opened the door and looked out, leading with his weapon. Then he saw it, on the concrete patio floor.

"Oh, no," he said. "A bird flew into the window." He stepped outside and took a closer look at the bird, which looked like a female robin. He put a tentative finger out and touched it and it fluttered its wings.

"I think she's only dazed," he said. He crouched down and watched the bird until it started trying to get up. Then he picked it up gingerly in his hands and carried it over to the edge of the patio and set it on the grass. It took it a couple of minutes to decide that it could fly. As soon as it flew away, he came back inside.

"She was terrified. But once she decided I wasn't going to kill her, she relaxed and caught her breath and finally was able to fly away." He was babbling because he didn't know what to say to Maddy.

While he'd been watching the bird, he'd thought about what he'd almost done. Again. It was a damn good thing the robin hit the door when it did, because every second he indulged himself with Maddy was another second he wasn't spending trying to find out who killed Tristan. Never mind that his resistance to her was crumbling like a stilt shack in an earthquake. Never mind that although he had no idea why, he was beginning to care for her in a deep, deep way he'd never cared about anyone before.

He couldn't afford to let her get to him. He needed to devote all his strength and focus to figuring out why Tristan was murdered and by whom. He didn't have enough of either to spare for selfish pleasure.

He turned to Maddy and thought about what she'd said just a few minutes before. "You said I got in your way," he said, his voice hard.

Maddy looked up at him in surprise. "I was mad," she began.

"What else were you going to say? That I got in your way and kissed you? That I got in your way and made love with you? I guess you're thinking that all that's distracting." He scowled at her. "Well, guess what, Maddy. You're getting in my way, too. You think I like it that I think about having sex with you when I ought to be figuring out what happened to Tristan? You think I enjoy being distracted by you while my oldest friend's killer goes free? I've only got until the end of this week before I have to be back at my job and I know little more than I did when I got here. All I've got is speculation."

He turned and looked out the French doors, knowing that if he kept looking at her while he tried to make her believe he didn't want or need her there, she'd see through him immediately. "So it works out perfectly that you're being taken off the case. In fact, it's a relief."

"A relief?" she said, the hurt in her voice evident. "Is that what you said?"

He didn't turn around. "Yes," he said just as her phone rang.

"Oh, hi, Brock. Thanks for calling me back." She listened for a moment. "I see. Sure. That makes sense. Of course. I'll be ready." She clicked the phone off and stood staring at it."

"Maddy?" Zach said. "What was that?"

"They denied my request. I can't stay. They've made a reservation for me for tomorrow morning on a commercial flight to DC. I have to drive to New Orleans this evening."

And that easily, he was let off the hook. He didn't have to explain that he didn't want her here, or that she was mistaken if she thought he needed her. He didn't have to look her in the eye and tell her the biggest lie of all, that it would be a lot easier to find out the truth about how Tristan died without her around.

She uttered a nervous laugh. "But I don't have a car."

He looked at her. "You can drive mine and leave it at the airport," he said.

Chapter Ten

When Maddy came out of her room a couple of hours later, after packing her clothes while tears streamed down her cheeks, Zach wasn't in the house. She figured he'd gone down to the dock as he'd said before he'd driven her half-crazy with need then told her he wanted her gone.

She still had on jeans and a T-shirt, so she decided she'd walk down to the dock, too. She wanted to see what was so interesting about it. Zach had told her to stay inside, but she had no further obligation to do anything he told her to except leave. So if he got upset because she went to the dock, then he could just lump it.

She headed down the path she'd seen him walk the other day. It wasn't much of a path. It was so overgrown with weeds and vines in a lot of places that it was difficult to tell whether there was a path there at all. She'd told him the truth when she'd said she'd never been in the swamp. This overgrown ground didn't exactly qualify as swamp, but as she walked, she could hear leaves rustling, twigs snapping and other sounds that had to come from animals. The sounds, coupled with her imagination, made her nervous. But she was determined.

Finally, just as the path seemed to disappear totally into tangled underbrush and she was two steps away from giving up and turning around, she saw a clearing up ahead. Relieved, she hurried toward it, then stopped, nervous about seeing Zach now that she was here. What would she say if he confronted her? Would he be mean to her again?

It was too late now. She was already here. She walked through the last of the undergrowth and out into the clearing and gasped. It was beautiful. She knew that cypress trees and oleander bushes were pretty, but she'd never paid that much attention to them. The rickety, weathered dock, the odd plants and flowers growing in the water and on land, air plants nestled in the crooks of the cypress limbs and the cypress knees forming gargoyle-like shapes in the water gave the small area an alien look. It was rustic and beautiful, and something, maybe the oleander, lent a sweet scent to the air.

Maddy stepped onto the weathered boards of the dock and walked out a little way, so that when she crouched down she could see the patterns in the mud made by at least one boat that had tied up to the dock recently. There wasn't much room on either side of the wooden boards to pull a boat aground. The vessel would have to be small. But in contrast, the water at the end of the dock was deep enough for a fair-size motorboat.

Straightening, she shaded her eyes and looked out over the Gulf, thinking about the *Pleiades Seagull*. It was about twenty-five miles offshore. A relatively small rig, it employed about four hundred workers, including the captain and his crew. It was in fairly shallow water and was drilling very deep. She wasn't familiar with the drill being used, but she did know that it was a proprietary design that was specially tooled to work on such a small platform in shallow waters.

Looking back at the mostly dried mud near the edge of the water, she wondered how deep it was and how hard. If she could walk out from shore just a yard or so, or maybe not even that far, she could get a better look at the patterns made by the boats and see if up close they looked as much like the textured bottom paint used on oil rig lifeboats as she thought they had from a distance. She needed to get a sample of the pattern, whether it was a broken crust of the hardened mud or a photo, so she could compare it closely with the lifeboats' bottom-paint texture.

She sat down on the dock and started to untie her sneakers.

"You oughtn't do that, you," a gruff voice said.

Maddy jumped and jerked her head around. "Who—" She saw an old man in worn pants and shirt, wearing a bedraggled fishing hat and carrying a shotgun that was as highly polished as any firearm in a museum. "Wh-who are you?" she asked.

"That's not important," the man said. "You best leave your shoes alone and get down off that dock. Anybody lives around here knows you can't get outta the gumbo mud once you get into it, I guarantee. So you ain't from here, you."

The man's words were sort of slurred and run together, but she didn't think it was from drinking. His hand trembled on the shotgun and he only talked out of one side of his mouth. His left eye looked as if it was permanently half-closed, too. He must have had a stroke.

"I don't live here," she said, trying to keep her voice steady as she slowly rose to her feet. She didn't think he would shoot her, but she couldn't be totally sure.

"That's right," he mumbled. "So what you

doing down here trying to get yourself stuck in the gumbo mud, you?"

She wiped her hands on her jeans and turned to step off the dock.

"You stay right there while we talk," he said.

She nodded. "Yes, sir. I came down here to look at the marks made by the boat that pulled in here, probably two days ago," she told him, gesturing back toward the mud.

"Three," he said.

"What? Excuse me?"

"Three days ago. Not days, nights. It was around midnight. The boat got its motor stuck in the mud. That motor's gone, I guarantee." The man chuckled. His shoulders shook with his muffled laughs.

"I could see that it had gotten stuck. It stirred up the mud a lot. Do you know who they were or what they were doing?" Maddy asked, hoping that his chuckling meant he'd tell her what she wanted to know.

"Nah," he said. "Nah. Me, I never saw them folks before. But I guarantee they don't know much about Louisiana mud nor Gulf water."

She nodded, smiled and glanced down at the ground, but thick, green grass was growing down to within a foot of the waterline.

"No footprints," the old man said. "You got some training, you?"

"I know a little bit about boats. You said the men didn't know much about mud or Gulf water?"

"That's right. They pulled and pushed and moaned and groaned to get them bags outta the boat and into the wagon, just a-sinking in the mud and slipping on the grass and them a-talking the whole time."

"What bags? What were they talking about?"

The man chuckled. "The bags, they was dark green. Looked like body bags. That tough canvas, you know?"

She nodded.

"What'd they talk about? Everything. Said something about a dry run. Dry run on water," he said and chuckled again. "Said if it went okay and the cap'n was happy, they'd bring two boats, maybe more, next time. The one guy, he said they gotta bring 'em during the new moon. The other man, he say the bogeyman come out in the dark of the moon. The one man, he laugh at him and say shut up and push the wagon."

"What kind of wagon?"

"Me, I don't know. A wagon's a wagon. See, the road now, it's so grown over that a truck can't get down here like it used to. So those men, they got to drag those heavy bags with a wagon all the way 'thout no help." He chuckled again. "The ground is rough and they lost some of their booty."

"Booty? What was the booty? What was in the bags?" Maddy had a hard time keeping her voice steady. Had the boat come from the oil platform and had the old man seen what was in the bags?

"They was heavy, I guarantee you that. They's probably smart to use body bags. I saw them boys sink to their ankles in the mud, and it was a treat to watch them try and get out. But they ended up okay."

"Did you pick up something that fell out of the bag?" Maddy asked, trying to draw the man's attention back to her without angering him.

"I guarantee you I did. You want to guess what they was carrying?"

"I'm sure I can't," she said sweetly, then held her breath. Would he tell her what they were smuggling?

The man let the shotgun's barrel drop as he reached into the pocket of his pants and drew out a handgun.

Maddy nearly gasped. From where she was standing, she didn't recognize the make, but she knew that she'd never seen a gun like it before. The handle was longer by at least an inch than any handgun she'd ever seen. It also had what looked like a long magazine sticking out of the handle. Extra bullets? She did her best to memorize what she saw. "Is that the only one you have?" she asked him.

"Nah. I picked up three."

"Would you let me have one?" she asked shakily. If she could get her hands on one of those guns, she just might have the answer to what Tristan had stumbled upon that had gotten him killed.

The old man stared at her, his head angled so he could see her with his one good eye. "What you want with a gun, girl?"

"I can shoot," she said. "I'm pretty good, and I'd love to have a gun like that. Have you shot it?"

He shook his head. "Nah. Ain't got no bullets. You got bullets?"

"No. I don't know what kind it takes, but if you'd let me have one, I can find some bullets for it. Then you and I can do some shooting at targets. Would you like to do that?"

He shrugged. "I ain't too keen on little guns," he said.

Maddy smiled at him again. "I can get you some shells for that shotgun, too, if you want me to."

"Yeah?" He thought a minute. "That'd be nice, I reckon." He looked at the handgun, then tossed it at her feet.

She bent and picked it up. A quick glance didn't help her at figuring out what it was, but it was heavy and not very well balanced. She could tell that just from holding it.

"Don't shoot yourself, girl."

"Hard to do without bullets," she threw back at him as she turned to leave.

"Hey," he said.

She stopped.

"You didn't ever tell me why you came down here, you. How'd you get down here to this old dock?" he asked, looking bewildered. "You looking for something?"

Maddy studied the man for a moment before she spoke. "I'm trying to find out why Tristan DuChaud was killed."

The old man took a step backward and raised his shotgun. "Girl oughtn't be down here. You don't go stirring up an alligator nest if you don't want to run into the mama gator. You understand me, you?"

Maddy didn't, but she nodded her head anyway. "Yes, sir," she said.

"Now, take that evil little gun and go on, you. Get outta here, and don't come back. Pretty *chér* like you get yourself hurt if you don't watch out." He sounded angry, but he lowered the gun. "Go on."

"Yes, sir," she said again, and half walked,

half ran back into the undergrowth. She kept jogging as long as she could without tripping over branches and vines. When she made it back to the house, she locked the French doors and took a long hot shower. To her dismay, she found three ticks crawling on her skin, looking for a place to dig in and feed.

By the time Maddy slipped on a pink-and-white caftan, there was a delicious aroma in the air and it was driving her tummy nuts. She hadn't eaten anything all day and she was starving. When she walked into the kitchen, Zach was stirring something in a pot on the stove.

"Mmm, do I smell jambalaya?" she asked, taking a deep whiff of the air.

He put the lid on the pot and turned around deliberately. "Where were you?"

She pointed vaguely back toward the bedrooms. "In the shower."

He growled under his breath. "I mean earlier. Around two o'clock."

"I went down to the boat dock. It's really beautiful down there, but a few ticks decided to have a picnic on me." She shuddered.

"I told you not to leave the house," he said. "When I couldn't find you I thought you might have left, until I looked in your room and saw your suitcases and your clothes."

"You must have been so angry that I didn't listen to you," she said blandly.

He glowered. "I wondered if you'd been kidnapped or hurt."

She shook her head. "Nope. Just exploring. I met the most interesting man."

"Man? Who?"

"I don't know his name. He wouldn't tell me. But he was an old Cajun man with a shotgun. He told me all about the gumbo mud and how I shouldn't step in it or I might not get out again."

"You talked to Boudreau?" Zach asked, sounding disbelieving.

"Is that his name? He told me some other things, too, very interesting things, and I found out a few things for myself."

Zach turned his back and stirred the pot again.

Maddy peeked around him to see what he was cooking. "Wow that smells good. Jambalaya is one of my favorite dishes in the entire world."

"It's from a mix," he said.

"Trust me. I do not care. It smells wonderful."

He banged the lid onto the pot, balanced the spoon on top of the lid, then turned back around. "Well? Are you going to tell me what you found?"

"Oh, right." She went to the kitchen table, trying not to think about what they'd just recently done on it, and turned on her tablet. "I've been checking the Gulf of Mexico sea charts for this area."

"Yeah?"

"Right there where Tristan's dock is, there is a long shallow shelf, then a drop-off."

"Yeah? That's not news. I grew up playing and boating around that dock."

"Right. Well, as it turns out, the lifeboats on the *Pleiades Seagull* could clear the shelf with one passenger, maybe two."

Zach's brows drew down. "How do you know that and what exactly does it mean?"

"I know because I'm an oil rig inspector and I know the specs of the *Seagull*'s lifeboats and I can read charts."

"Okay," he said, looking a little confused. "And it means...?"

"It means that the same boat, full of cargo, would run aground if someone tried to put its bow in to shore."

"I think a boat ran aground there last week, based on what I saw down at the dock," he said, looking more interested now that he was probably beginning to understand what she was getting at.

She nodded. "I think so, too."

"You think it was loaded with cargo?"

She nodded again.

He checked the jambalaya, stirred it one last

time, then turned off the gas. "We can eat in a few minutes," he said. "I wish I knew what they were carrying and why they brought it to Tristan's little dock."

"Do you?" she asked. "Because I could make that wish come true."

Chapter Eleven

"What the hell are you doing, Maddy. If you know something that would help figure out what really happened to Tristan, tell me."

"I'm getting to it. Boudreau told me."

Zach crossed his arms and shook his head. "Boudreau? You met Boudreau? You need to understand that he's not exactly running on all cylinders."

"I didn't get that impression at all."

"When I talked to him he was talking to himself. When he finally said something to me it didn't make a whole lot of sense. You noticed the way his mouth and eye droops, didn't you? Duff told me he's had a stroke."

"Why don't you listen to what he said to me, and then you can tell me what you think. Boudreau told me that some folks who didn't know what they were doing tried to bring a boat up onto shore at Tristan's dock, but it got stuck and they didn't have any better sense than to get out in the gumbo mud and try to pull it up onto shore."

"He saw them?"

"That's what he said. But according to him, they finally got the bags onto shore with some help. They put the bags on a wagon."

Zach uncrossed his arms and started pacing between the table and the French doors. After about three round-trips, he stopped. "Did he tell you anything about the bags?"

"He said they were heavy, like body bags, and stuffed full."

"Heavy," Zach said, rubbing a hand across his cheeks and chin. "Did he see what was in them?"

Maddy got up to fetch the weapon. As she picked up the small bag, a lump grew in her throat. She was about to show Zach what Tristan had died for. She presented it to him solemnly. "This," she said. "This is what they're smuggling."

He took the bag and she could tell by his face that he knew immediately what he was holding. He pulled out the handgun and looked at it, then at her, then looked at it again more closely. He studied it, ejected the magazine, checked that it was empty, reinserted it, then laid it down on the table. "That's an automatic," he muttered.

Maddy nodded. "I finally figured that out," she said.

"I mean an *automatic*," he repeated. "Not a semiautomatic. If you pull that trigger, you'll fire at least three rounds."

"I know," she said.

He looked up at her from beneath his brows. "How did Boudreau get this?"

"He said it fell off the wagon. From what I understood him to say, he had three, until he gave me this one."

Zach sat there and stared at the gun for a long time. He blinked occasionally and once or twice he cleared his throat and rubbed his eyes. Finally he looked up at her again. "He gave it to you? Did he know who you are?"

"Yes, he did, and no, he didn't."

"Do you know what this means?"

She nodded, pressing her lips together and blinking her stinging eyes. "Yes. I do."

He shook his head. "This is why Tristan was killed. This is what he heard. He heard them talking about smuggling automatic handguns into the US." He slammed a fist down on the table. "Why couldn't he have told someone?" he shouted. "Damn it, Tristan. Why?"

LATE THAT AFTERNOON, Maddy was finishing packing to leave and Zach was sitting on the picnic table arguing with himself about the best thing to do regarding the automatic handguns, when his phone rang. When he answered, it was his boss, Bill. He didn't even give Zach a chance to say hello before he launched into a tirade. In fact, Zach missed the beginning.

"—if I'd thought that was what you were doing. Damn it, Winter. What the hell's going on down there? As soon as I get off this phone I'm ordering a helicopter to pick you up and you're going to wish you'd never heard of NSA. Your butt is going to be stamped NSA, Non-Secure-Ass."

Zach groaned inwardly at the old inside joke. "Bill, what are you talking about?"

"You shut up and listen to me."

There was a lot of static on the line and Zach was afraid he was going to lose the connection. "Bill. Bill! Hold on. There's only one place around here I can get a signal. Hold on!" He hurried inside and went into the nursery. "Okay. I can hear you now. I missed most of what you said after you told me to shut up."

"Listen to me, Zach. I want you to get down to the sheriff's office right this minute because I don't want to have to go over it all again with you. You can get it from the sheriff."

"Get what?"

Bill went on as if Zach hadn't spoken. "I've

been on the phone all day, first with the Coast Guard, then with the sheriff, and then with Homeland Security."

Zach winced. He knew that there had been a rivalry between Bill at NSA and one of the chief deputy directors at Homeland Security for years, and he knew how seriously Bill took that rivalry. He hadn't told Bill about Maddy. So who did? Hell, it was probably his archrival deputy director, trying to one-up him.

"The next time you decide to take a vacation and climb into bed with Homeland Security, could you please give me a heads-up?"

"Into bed?" Zach said hoarsely before he realized that Bill was using the term metaphorically.

Bill obviously heard Zach's tone. "Oh, come on, Zach. Please don't tell me you've been—"

"Bill!" Zach interrupted. "Slow down. I have no idea what you're talking about." He heard plastic rattling as Bill pulled a cigarette out of the ever-present pack in his pocket. Then he heard a match strike and Bill's long inhalation. He knew that within a few seconds his boss would be a little more calm and a lot more rational.

"Okay. Yeah. We've been picking up chatter from some rigs in the Gulf of Mexico for months now. There are oil rigs that are doing double duty as smuggling rings for domestic terrorist groups, survivalists and other fringe organizations and, of course, organized crime. At least one of those rigs has access to automatic handguns. *Automatics*, Zach. Think about that. Word is they're starting to show up in some metropolitan areas in the South, in the hands of *kids*."

"Yeah," Zach said with a sigh.

Bill kept talking. "According to Homeland Security, a couple months ago they zeroed in on the *Pleiades Seagull* as the primary source for the chatter. Zach, your friend DuChaud must have discovered that the talk about the weapons was coming from the *Pleiades Seagull*."

"I know."

"I knew it!" Bill cried. "For Pete's sake. Are you the one who called in the tip to the Coast Guard? Have you found any evidence in DuChaud's house? What have you been doing—"

"Bill," Zach said.

"I don't get it, Zach. You could have requested the assignment. You wouldn't have gotten it. It's a conflict of interest, but you had an obligation as an NSA agent to let me know what you'd discovered. Why didn't you? I'd have assigned an agent—"

"Bill!" Zach yelled. "Shut up!"

"I— What?"

"Shut up for a minute. First of all, no! I did not call in any tip. I don't know anything about a tip.

And I didn't know anything for certain about smuggling until just two hours ago. I heard, secondhand, that someone witnessed a boat coming ashore and off-loading two large bags that apparently contained firearms. And yes, they are automatics. Judging by what I've been told, I'm guessing there could be scores of them, maybe even hundreds. The sketchy information I got didn't mention where the boat came from nor where they took the bags. I have a good idea where they were taken, but I can't verify it because *I just found out*!"

"Okay, okay," Bill said. "Who gave you the information? And do you know if they called the Coast Guard? Are you sure you didn't know anything about this?"

"I got the information from a—" Zach decided not to bring up Homeland Security or Maddy. Not until he had to. He didn't want Bill to know his metaphor about being in bed with Homeland Security was literally true. Not yet.

It was obvious that within the past few hours a lot of stuff had hit the fan. He was going to need some time to separate the facts from the speculation. So he kept his explanation generic, with no names. "From a woman who heard it from an old Cajun man who's old and probably has had a stroke, so not the most reliable witness of anything. I haven't talked to the Coast

Guard or the sheriff because I have no evidence of anything. Least of all whether Tristan fell off the rig or was pushed."

There was a long pause, during which Zach listened to Bill inhale. "Well, what the hell are you doing down there if you're not investigating this smuggling thing? Why were you so hot to take a week's vacation?"

"Because I needed to find out the truth about how Tristan died. It looks like I'm the last one to know." He looked up to see Maddy at the door, her eyes wide. *Are you okay?* she mouthed.

He nodded and turned away from her.

"So what now?" Bill asked.

"I guess I'm going to go down to the sheriff's office. Tell me about the tip."

Bill sighed. "Can't you ask the sheriff? I already—"

"Bill!"

"Okay, okay. The call came in from an unknown cell phone that was tracked to a tower near Bonne Chance. Do you know how few towers there are in that area?"

"Tell me about it. I'm standing in what may be the only place on this side of Bonne Chance where I can get a signal. But you're saying the phone call came from around here?"

"That's what I was told. They couldn't get a reliable triangulation. I doubt we'll ever figure out who called unless they come forward. Of course, all our calls to NSA are recorded and reviewed. The ones that may have to do with national security are flagged."

"I know," Zach said through clenched teeth. "I work there."

Maddy was still standing at the door, damn her. If she had decent hearing at all, she could hear Bill. The man had a shrill tenor voice. He'd never had a private conversation in his life because his voice carried as if it were being broadcast over gigantic loudspeakers.

"This was one of those calls. It came in around eight o'clock this morning. I'm going to play it. Listen."

"Put it on speaker," Maddy said.

Too irritated to argue, Zach punched the speaker button.

After several clicks and some static, he heard a voice. It was raspy and low. Zach listened closer. It was a lot like Boudreau's voice, except that it didn't sound old or crazy. *Don't hang up. I got good information. There's an oil rig—Pleiades Seagull. The captain is planning to... smuggle guns. Can't say when or where, but he's got to be stopped. People going to die. People already died.* There was another, final-sounding click on the line and it went dead.

"Well?" Bill said.

"Well what?" Zach retorted.

"Do you know who it is?"

"It sounds like the Cajun man I mentioned, but that guy isn't responsible for his actions. He's had a stroke. You can't trust anything he says."

"That's not true!" Maddy cried.

Zach held up his hand and glared at her.

"I'm going to assume that's Homeland Security in the background and I'm going to ignore her."

Zach didn't comment.

"So what are you going to do?"

"Well, Bill, you're my boss. What do you want me to do?"

"I want you to go see the sheriff and then I want both of you to talk to the Coast Guard and figure out the best course of action. Figure out how to find out whether the guns are on the rig yet and when and how they're going to be moved ashore and where they're going after that. And then I want you to *stop them*!"

Zach shook his head. His jaw hurt, he'd been clenching it for so long. "No problem, boss, I'll get right on it," he said grudgingly. "I guess I'm off vacation." And he hung up.

As soon as he hit the off button, Maddy was on him. "Boudreau is not crazy. Have you forgotten what I told you he said about the guns and the boats? He was right. Why didn't you tell your boss that Boudreau thinks the guns will be moved tonight."

"Because Boudreau is not competent. I talked to him, Maddy."

"Well, where do you think he got those guns?"

"In the first place, you don't know if he has more than one. And I'll grant you, it's entirely possible that he found it somewhere around the dock. You and I both know that someone in a heavy boat got grounded there."

"What he said makes sense," Maddy insisted.

Zach shook his head. "I can't go by the word of an old man who at best has had a major stroke. He stood there holding that shotgun on me and telling me I'm the devil and he can't look me in the eye. And he didn't know me. Said he'd never seen me before. No. He's a crazy old man who has no idea what he's talking about."

"Who was that on the recording?" she pushed.

"How the hell do I know. Like I told Bill, it sounded like Boudreau if Boudreau wasn't a hundred years old, sick and, by the way, crazy."

"So what did he say?" she asked. "Your boss."

"You heard most of it. He told me about the tip. That's basically it. Apparently, they'd already brought in a small load of guns, which is where Boudreau got the one he gave you. Kind of a dry run. We've been hearing chatter for months about automatic handguns. The idea is to give them to everybody from organized crime to punk kids and who knows who else. I hate to think about what will happen to New Orleans or Galveston or Houston if those guns are distributed all over. It could be devastating for the lower-income neighborhoods." He rubbed his forehead. "I can see it now. Teens getting shot. Little kids. Those streets will turn into bloodbaths."

"Oh, no. It could be catastrophic," Maddy said with a gasp. "Zach, do you have any idea how many guns were in each of those bags? Boudreau said two guys struggled with the weight. Each bag probably had fifty guns or more."

Maddy was pale, and Zach knew exactly how she felt. Fifty per bag, two bags per boat, who knew how many boat trips. That many small automatic weapons could raise gun violence in the United States dramatically. Enough boatloads of them and the dynamic between the criminal community and law enforcement could be changed forever. Or at least until every cop and every criminal was carrying an automatic. He shook his head. "We've got to stop the guns."

"But how? We need to catch them in the act."

Zach nodded. "The call said the *Pleiades Seagull*'s captain is involved."

She nodded. "That's exactly what Tristan

thought. He said the incriminating conversations he heard were between the captain and someone who was apparently very high up in the company."

"Did you say Boudreau heard what the two men were saying while they unloaded the guns?"

She nodded. "They said if the trial run went well and if the captain approved, they'd bring the big shipment in two boats or maybe more. He said they planned to do it during the new moon, which is tonight. We should go talk to him. He gets around in that swamp without making a sound. He's probably seen or heard something else."

Zach looked up, his face haggard. "*We* aren't doing anything. *You* are leaving."

Maddy felt as though he'd slapped her. She shouldn't have expected him to change his mind, but she had. That's how naive she was. She'd actually thought for a little while that he cared for her. She knew better now and she would know better for the rest of her life.

Men like him didn't fall for women like her. She'd been a convenient distraction. That was all. "Oh. Don't worry. I am," she said stiffly. "In just a few minutes. I guess you're going to see the sheriff and talk to the Coast Guard?"

He grimaced and ran his thumbnail along the

corner of his bottom lip, as she'd seen him do time after time when he was thinking or if he was unsure about something. "Maybe," he said.

"Zach," she said, wiping her hands down the sides of her jeans. "Thanks."

He looked up at her from beneath his brows. "For what?"

She shrugged. "Oh, you know, everything." Then she turned and headed for her room. As she turned the doorknob, she looked back over her shoulder. He was closing the door to the nursery, Sandy's car keys in his hand.

"Be careful, Zach," she said.

His gaze slid from hers down to the keys he held, then back up. He nodded and right at the end of the nod, the corner of his mouth turned up. "I will." He strode up the hall. At the kitchen door, he stopped and turned.

"Maddy? You, too," he said, then headed through the French doors out to Sandy's car.

Maddy stood there at the door to the guest room until she heard the car's smooth engine rumble to life, then hum as Zach put it in gear and drove away. As she listened to the sound fade in the distance, she closed her eyes and bit her lip.

She was not going to cry anymore. Who was Zach Winter that he deserved her tears? Nobody. That was who. So why was she wasting them on him? A small voice deep inside her whispered, *Because you know he's worth all the tears you can cry.*

"Oh, shut up," she snapped at that small voice. She pushed the guest room door open and saw her suitcases on the bed. Sighing, she remembered that she had to finish packing and get out of here. Zach had told her to leave. She looked around the room, trying to figure out what she'd forgotten. Then she remembered that she'd left her shampoo and conditioner in the master bath. She'd been showering in there to avoid Zach, who was using the hall bath.

When she pushed open the door to the master bedroom, she came face-to-face with a stranger. He was holding one of the automatic handguns.

WHEN ZACH WALKED into the sheriff's office, Sheriff Baylor Nehigh, or Barley, as he was called in high school, turned and shook his head at Zach, every bit as if he were the disappointed principal whom the teacher had sent Zach to for punishment. "Zach, you and me, we know each other." Barley had a plug of tobacco in his cheek and he paused to spit into a coffee can. "I was in the same grade as your sister, Zoe, back when you were a skinny kid with a big chip on your shoulder. Seemed like no matter what you did, you were always trying to do it better than anybody else. I guess you still are. How come I had to find out who you work for from your boss instead of you?"

"I'm sure he told you I came down here for Tristan's funeral. I wasn't on assignment or in any kind of official capacity."

"You saying you didn't have to notify me?"

Zach sighed. "No, I'm not saying that. I'm saying all I was doing was trying to find out if there was any proof that Tristan didn't accidentally fall and drown."

"All right. What have you found out?"

"Not much. But I can tell you Tristan didn't fall."

"But can you prove it?"

Zach shook his head.

"So how much of what your boss told me did you already know?" Barley spit again.

"None of it. I mean, I did find out that there was chatter being picked up about some of the oil rigs down here. Apparently, Homeland Security—"

Barley held up his hand. "I know that Madeleine Tierney is with Homeland Security and that Tristan was, too. I'm disappointed in Tristan that he didn't let me know what he was doing. I'd like to think I could have done something to help."

"Have you talked to the Coast Guard?" Zach

asked. "Have they picked up the captain or started the evacuation of the platform?"

"They're going to start evacuating the platform sometime this afternoon. I got a report about an hour ago that they can't find the captain. I reckon he jumped ship. They said there was one lifeboat missing. But apparently, not one person saw or heard him leave. Not one."

Zach closed his eyes as the sound of chewing tobacco hitting the side of the metal can rang in the air. "The captain's not on the rig? We've got to find him. Maddy said that Tristan had talked about overhearing and/or recording at least one, maybe more, telephone conversations between the captain and some big shot who was apparently giving the orders about moving the weapons."

Barley nodded. "Well, that figures. So he and Miss Maddy knew that the captain was involved and yet didn't come to me?"

Zach stood and started to pace. "What are you getting at, Barley? Why all the complaints that nobody came to you?"

"Look, Winter. I'm more than willing to help out. But you got to remember, this is a small town. I don't have but one deputy and today he's off up to Houma, taking them some papers and picking some up." Barley spit, then held up his hands. "I know what you're thinking. But the reason I can't send that stuff by email is them not us. It's the parish clerks. They don't have their data on the computer yet."

Zach turned on his heel and started back toward the sheriff. "The only thing I'm thinking is what's the Coast Guard doing and when are the smugglers going to bring more guns in? Maddy thought it might be tonight."

"Tonight, eh? What's Homeland Security's plan?"

"My boss told me they're sending a couple of people to help us out, but they won't get here until tomorrow."

"Tomorrow? What's the holdup?"

"I get the feeling they're sending them via commercial airliner. They could send them down here in no time in a helicopter, but that's a lot more expensive."

"That's the government for you. They don't give a rat's ass that one of their own got killed?"

"I'm sure they do," Zach said, ignoring the fact that he'd thought the same thing. "Homeland Security has to consider more than just the life of one agent. They are, as you know, responsible for the safety of the entire country. Look, Barley, I'm going to head over to Tristan's dock. That's where they're going to bring the guns in because that dock is closest to the seafood warehouse.

"What's that got to do with anything?" the sheriff asked.

"The warehouse is the perfect place for them to bring the guns to load them for shipment. They could have an eighteen-wheeler in there and nobody would know. I need to know who your contact is with the Coast Guard."

Barley looked at his phone. "Captain David Reasoner. Here's his cell number. You can reach him if he's not too far out from shore."

"Thanks. Keep the smuggling thing quiet if you can."

Barley sent him a glowering look. "I can. See that you do."

As he drove back to Tristan's house, Zach dialed Captain Reasoner.

"Reasoner." The name was clipped, the tone slightly impatient.

Zach told him who he was and what he wanted to know. "If you need to, you can call my immediate superior. NSA Deputy Assistant Director Bill Wetzell."

"No need. We've already spoken," Reasoner said. "We radioed the *Pleiades Seagull* this morning at 0800. I asked to speak with Captain Poirier just to see how things were going. I do that routinely. The captain was unavailable, according to his first mate. When I asked if there was a problem, he said that they'd had an internal issue yesterday that had kept the captain up all night and that he was sleeping."

Zach didn't interrupt. He just listened.

"One of my crew noticed that there was a lifeboat missing. I asked the first mate about that and he said that was part of the incident. That it had been damaged and they'd taken it down so no one would try to use it in an emergency."

"What do you think, Captain?" Zach asked when he'd finished.

"I don't think the captain is aboard. I also don't think the lifeboat was damaged. I started to ask to see the damaged boat but decided not to push it at that time. However, I am considering going back there, boarding the platform and having a look for myself. I don't like the evasion. Particularly since their communications expert died last week. Your boss, Deputy Assistant Director Wetzell, told me that the *Pleiades Seagull* has been targeted as a source for some anti-American chatter."

"That's the word I got," Zach agreed. "In fact, judging by several factors, including some anecdotal evidence, I'm expecting there to be contraband moved from the platform to shore tonight. Think you'd be able to spare any men to help catch these guys in the act?"

"It would be my pleasure, Agent Winter."

Chapter Twelve

Maddy tried to scream, but no sound came out of her mouth. She clutched at her throat and tried to catch her breath as the man came closer. "Who—" she rasped, still not able to force much sound past her fear-constricted throat.

"Shut up," the man said and slapped her face with his empty hand.

Maddy fell sideways, onto one knee and one palm. She gasped, partly in pain and partly in outrage, and vaulted to her feet. The side of her face stung and tingled, but the shock of the blow loosened her throat. "Who are you and what are you doing in this house?"

She took a closer look at the man. "Wait a minute. I know you. You're Captain Poirier from the *Pleiades Seagull*. What are you doing in here? Get out. This is a private residence and you need to—"

He swung at her again. She ducked, but the edge of his hand caught her chin. She staggered but stayed on her feet. Stars danced before her eyes and the anger inside her exploded. "Stop it!" she snapped. "Do *not* hit me again."

"Then stop talking," he said, taking a threatening step toward her and raising his hand again. "I need you to do something for me."

"What's going on here? How did you—" As she took another step backward, she glanced toward the window and saw that it was open. He'd opened it through a hole the intruders had cut. "You sent them, didn't you?"

"I told you to—"

"I know," she said, smiling in spite of the ringing pain in her head. "I'll be quiet, but please, don't hit me again." Silently she added, *Or I might have to hurt you.* She was contemplating what she could do to either take the man down or talk him into letting her go. "Captain, is there something I can do for you?" she asked as she used her peripheral vision to search for something in Sandy's room that could be used as a weapon.

She realized he was going to grab her about a fifth of a second before he lunged toward her, which wasn't quite enough time for her to react. He grabbed her by one arm, squeezing inside the elbow until it went limp and throbbed with pain. "Now, see if you can keep that mouth shut for a few minutes or I'll have to find a rag to stuff in it." He twisted her arm a little. Just enough to make her cry out.

Digging into his pocket again, he came out with a large plastic tie that looked like the ones on food bags, except about a hundred times the size. He grabbed her right wrist and looped the tie around it. "Now turn around. *Slowly*. Don't try anything or I'll make you think that so far we've been having a picnic. Got that?"

Maddy nodded meekly and turned around slowly. If she had her gun, or a pair of scissors or even a nail file, she could defend herself and possibly even manage to get away. But she had nothing. All she could do was stand there as he fastened her wrists together behind her.

"That's too tight," she said.

"I told you to *shut up*!" he groused and shook her, hard. He half dragged, half walked her up the hall to the kitchen. "Where are your car keys?"

"Car keys?" Maddy repeated.

Poirier whirled and punched her in the stomach so fast and so hard that she doubled over, then collapsed onto the floor in pain. With her arms tethered behind her, she couldn't sit up or stand. All she could do was lie there and cough and try not to throw up.

Poirier lifted her up by her arms, nearly pulling them out of their sockets. He held on to her upper arms and shook her hard. Her eyes watered with pain and nausea. "Stop," she whispered. "Stop."

"Listen to me. I know that you are not as dumb as you're pretending to be. If you keep acting like a child, I will treat you like a child. Do you understand what that means?"

Maddy blinked hard. She didn't know what he wanted her to do. Should she answer him or just move her head without speaking?

"Do you? Look at me. I'm tired of hitting you with my hands. I've got a nice heavy buckle on my belt. I can use it on you until you can't move. It's how I disciplined my own kids until my wife left me. And it's how I'll discipline you. Got it?"

She nodded, which made her head hurt.

"I don't like to do that, you understand. But sometimes it has to be done. Now." He straightened his jacket and shot his shirt cuffs as if he were wearing a tuxedo. "Where are your car keys?"

Maddy was still having trouble breathing. Her throat and lungs were spasming from the shock and pain of his latest blow. She gestured shakily in the direction of the kitchen counter. She didn't bother to tell him they were Zach's keys, not hers.

Poirier picked up the keys and glared at her. "Let's go. You're riding in the trunk."

She walked outside on shaky legs. When he pressed the remote unlock on the car, then looked at the electronic key for a second and pressed the trunk release, she just stood there, staring at the car's trunk and trying to think. What did she know about the trunks of cars these days? Newer cars had a trunk release on the inside.

She averted her eyes from the trunk and from Poirier. But when he grabbed her by the arm and pulled her toward him, causing her to stumble, he laughed.

"You don't think I'm going to let you get into the trunk until I've taken care of the interior release, do you?" He took the gun he still held and slammed the butt into the small lever, then did it again. The little piece of metal broke and skittered along the metal wall of the trunk with a tinkling sound.

Then he jerked her over to stand in front of the open trunk. "Get in," he said.

She looked at the high interior edge of the trunk, which came to her hips, then looked at him.

"Lift your leg and throw it over the edge, you idiot," he said. When she didn't move immediately, he pushed the barrel of the gun into her side. "Did you notice what kind of gun I have? If not, I'll tell you. It's an automatic. That's right.

Can you imagine what it will do to you if I pull the trigger and hold it?"

She nodded. She lifted her left leg, trying to brace her tethered arm against the fender.

With a frustrated growl, Poirier pushed her in and shoved her right leg inside, then slammed the trunk lid.

Maddy closed her eyes. Her left arm hurt where she'd hit the edge of a metal tool case as she landed.

Poirier had twisted her knee when he'd stuffed her inside. It throbbed with pain. But while they hurt, her arm and leg were not what she was concerned about. She was afraid that wherever Poirier was taking her, he intended to kill her. And she didn't want to die.

She wanted to live. She regretted giving up so easily when Zach told her he didn't want her there with him. She wanted to go back there. Wanted one more chance. Next time, she'd fight to stay. She'd tell Brock that she wanted vacation and she'd glue herself to Zach's side until he couldn't deny that they had a connection that could not be ignored—*if* she had another chance.

She and Zach could be working together right now to bring Poirier down. She smiled at the image that rose before her vision of the two of them together, perfectly in tune. Two days ago, she hadn't even known Zach Winter. But now she knew that they were better together than either of them were alone. When they stood together, they were unstoppable. They always would be. She knew that. And so did he.

They would win, as long as they fought together.

Then she tried to move her leg, which was cramping, but she had no room since she was stuffed into the trunk of the car. She almost laughed. Sure. How easy was it to rethink the things she'd done. Easy to convince herself that Zach would have acquiesced, now that there was no way to find out. No way to ever go back and make things different.

All she knew for sure was that the end of this ride was probably going to be the end of her.

AFTER ZACH HUNG UP, he dialed Maddy's cell phone, but she didn't answer. When he got back to the house, his car was gone. Zach parked and stared at the empty space, then looked at his watch. If she'd showered and dried her hair before she left, she might not have been gone but about five or maybe ten minutes. He remembered her telling him she did a pretty fast shower. He smiled and tried her phone again.

"Come on, Maddy. Answer." Maybe she was one of those people who were adamant about not talking on the phone while driving. This time, he left a message. "Call me as soon as you get this, Maddy. If you haven't gone too far, you might want to turn back. It looks like it will all go down tonight, and I'd—I'd like to have you here, with me, if you want to be. Call me."

He hung up and put his phone in his pocket. For a second, he thought about going inside and waiting, in case she called right back. But there wasn't much time and he wanted to find Boudreau and get some answers about what he'd seen, then talk to Captain Reasoner again to nail down specific plans before it got dark. So he walked on down to the dock.

He looked around and called for Boudreau, but he didn't hear or see anything. So he examined the ground and the mud. There, in the few places where the overgrown grass and vines gave way to a muddy patch right around the water's edge, he saw recent tracks of a skinny, possibly metal, wheel. He turned and walked directly away from the dock, searching the ground. Sure enough, there were more wheel marks. He took a few flash photos of the marks with his phone and labeled, dated and initialed them in the device. He knew the courts were strict on entering digital photos into evidence, and at least he had them saved and annotated, just in case.

When he looked at one of the photos, the flash had produced shadows, enough that he could see the faint outline of a footprint alongside the metal wheel track. He took another couple of shots before he continued following the wheel tracks. Within another couple of hundred yards, he was out of the underbrush and in the sparsely grassed back of the old seafood warehouse.

He nodded. That's what he'd thought. The way that Maddy described what Boudreau had told her, the two men had pushed the wagon through the underbrush toward the warehouse. Boudreau had been convinced that's where they were going.

He walked around the building, checking out the entrances and looking at the ground. Sure enough, the thin metal wheel tracks went around to the freight door in front. He crouched down and looked at the door-lift mechanism. A few tufts of grass were caught there. Then Zach touched them. They were supple and nearly fresh. They must have gotten caught within the past two days.

Satisfied that he had enough information to let Captain Reasoner and the Coast Guard know what was likely going down in a few hours, Zach called him back and explained the layout. Reasoner immediately fired back with a simple and effective plan that was very close to what

Zach was thinking and told Zach he'd be able to give him three Coast Guard officers to capture the smugglers.

Reasoner told Zach he'd arranged for an ambulance with paramedics hidden in an empty car repair shop near the warehouse, if needed. A Coast Guard helicopter was also on call.

After arranging to meet Reasoner just after dark at the dock, Zach walked back that way and called Maddy again. He was able to hear her phone ring four times before the connection was lost. He walked out to the end of the dock, out from under any overhanging trees, and tried again.

That time, the phone rang until voice mail picked up. "Maddy, call me back," he said, standing perfectly still. He didn't want to lose the connection until he'd left his message. "I want to make sure you're okay. Try to call before dark, okay? We're hoping to catch the smugglers tonight. The Coast Guard's working with me."

He paused, rubbing his thumb across his lower lip. He knew how badly he'd hurt her when he'd told her he didn't need or want her around. And he knew how much of a bold-faced lie it was.

He still didn't want her here, for her own safety, although he knew he wasn't giving her the credit she deserved as a trained Homeland

Security agent. But he couldn't help it. He wasn't sure what he'd do if something happened to her.

Without understanding his reasoning, he said, "Truthfully, I'd feel better if you were here beside me. We make a good team."

He hung up, but he stood there for a minute, looking at the phone. *Call, Maddy. I know it's silly, but I'm worried about you.*

MADDY FELT AS THOUGH she couldn't breathe. It wasn't rational. But then, she was locked in the trunk of the car. What about that made sense?

There was plenty of air. She could feel it on her face. She could *see* the waning sunlight shining through the glass of the taillights. At least he hadn't blindfolded her or put a sack or a cloth over her head or gagged her. Thank goodness for the small stuff.

On the other hand, she was trussed and stuffed into the trunk of a car, everything hurt except her hands and that was *not* a good thing, and she was terrified.

Her eyes began to sting and she sniffed. "Oh, damn it," she whispered. She was crying. Why did she always have to cry? She hated it. There was no point to it. Crying was just a reflex left over from infancy, when it was the only way to get attention or food or a diaper change. And now her nose was running and it was even harder to breathe. Every time she sniffed she got a nose full of dust, carpet fibers and dirt.

It was almost funny. She was very likely about to die and what she was wishing for was a tissue.

She forced the whirling, panic-driven thoughts out of her brain. She had to focus. She zeroed in on the pale light coming through the red glass of the taillights. *Glass.* She'd heard of people locked in trunks kicking out taillights and waving and shouting until someone called the police and saved them. Had she seen that on a news show or a sitcom? Didn't matter. It was still worth a try. But when Maddy tried to scoot around to get her feet in position to kick the taillight out, she discovered that she really could not move. Her slight claustrophobia began to grow into full-blown panic.

At that very instant, the car stopped.

A rush of adrenaline streaked through her. It was a combination of relief and terror. But it did its job. They called it the fight-or-flight response. Her mind was suddenly clear and focused. Gone was the whimpering, helpless child.

Her knowledge and training, along with the innate human fight for survival, gave her the determination she needed. She had to figure out a strategy for dealing with Poirier if she wanted to survive.

She concentrated on her hands. They were totally numb and cuffed behind her back, so she had no idea whether her fingers were moving or not, but she willed them to flex and move and strain against the plastic strip. A searing pain in her wrists made her gasp and echoed through every muscle in her body. She'd seen characters in cop shows contort their bodies to get their hands under their legs and in front of them, then use friction to get out of a plastic handcuff. Just as she reminded herself that she couldn't move, the car door slammed, sending a shudder through the whole vehicle.

So much for Houdini-like escapes. If she'd wanted to do this the easy way, she'd have been sawing the plastic against one of those sharp edges sticking into her back the whole time Poirier was driving. It was too late now.

Poirier opened the trunk. Sunlight blazed in, forcing Maddy's burning eyes shut. She tried to squint, but the brightness was too much. Where was so much glare coming from? Her eyes still didn't want to open, so she had to force her eyelids to part for a fraction of a second at a time. Something in front of her—a huge building or wall—was reflecting the full strength of the sun.

Poirier grabbed her under her arms and dragged her bodily out of the trunk and set her upright. She swayed and took a stumbling step to lean against the fender while her head labored to adjust to being upright. The muscles in her legs cramped and she nearly fell. Just one more crippling pain to add to all the rest.

"Let's go," Poirier growled. "I don't want to take a chance on somebody seeing us. And if you try to scream, I'll knock all your teeth down your throat. Understand?"

Maddy nodded, her mind still working to figure out where they were. As her eyes adapted to the brightness, she saw that the glare was coming from a large, rust-streaked metal building.

Poirier stepped up to a garage door and pulled on the handle. It screeched and grated as metal slid over metal.

Maddy yawned to pop her ears after the auditory onslaught. Behind her back, she was still working her fingers and wrists. At least she hoped her hands were obeying her brain. She didn't want them to be numb when and if she was able to escape the plastic tie and needed to defend herself.

"Get in here," he ordered her. She hurried through the open freight door, unwilling to anger him again. She didn't think he would shoot her, but at this point she had no doubt that he would beat her with his belt buckle, and she couldn't stand the thought of that.

When she stepped inside the building,

the smell overwhelmed her. She gagged and coughed. It smelled like rotting shrimp shells and dead fish and iodine. It had to be the seafood warehouse. Boudreau had told her this was where they were bringing the guns. He was right.

Her eyes started watering and she coughed again. Blinking, she did her best to push past the smell so she could concentrate on taking in and remembering everything.

The first thing she noticed was the wagon Boudreau had described to her the other day. It had two large bags in it. Boudreau had said they were body bags. *The guns.*

Poirier jerked her over to the opposite wall and opened a door. Inside the dark room, Maddy thought she could make out a glint of pale light on porcelain. A toilet. It was a bathroom.

He shoved her inside and she heard a metallic rattling then a click, like a padlock. With the door closed, the room was pitch-black. And again, Maddy was trapped in a dark closed space. But this was worse by far than the car's trunk and the warehouse combined. Not only was it almost totally black, but it was hot and the smell had her gagging again. Right now, she'd be happy to breathe in the disgusting but identifiable odor of the warehouse.

This tiny closet should be giving off acid-green steam, the smell was so bad. It actually burned her throat and nose and eyes. And with her arms behind her back, there was nothing she could do about it. She did her best not to cough, because it would cause her to suck in even more putrid air.

Rather than give in to the nausea and pain and hopelessness of her situation, she worked on narrowing the focus of her existence down to one goal. One thing. Finding some light in the unrelenting darkness. She searched until finally, between the bottom of the door and the floor, she saw a needle-thin glow. It was only a couple of millimeters thick and was almost too pale to be seen, but it was enough. Her head quit whirling and she was able to orient herself in the world.

Unwilling to touch anything around her, she stood, trying not to sway or lose her sense of balance in the dark, fetid space. In desperation, she turned her concentration to a game she'd invented during DHS training, when she was forced to sit or hide in a bunker for long periods of time. She called it Name That Sound. It was an exercise aimed at using all her senses. Right now, she couldn't use her eyes or her sense of touch, so she concentrated on her hearing and her sense of smell.

She heard a car being cranked, heard the engine rev, then listened as it got louder. Poirier, or someone, was pulling a vehicle into the warehouse. It had to be Zach's car. The next sound after the engine stopped and a car door slammed was that metallic screech of the freight door being opened or lowered. She made an educated assumption that it was being lowered, since the only time she'd heard it before was when Poirier raised it.

Soon she smelled car exhaust. It actually surprised and dismayed her that she could smell the exhaust over the resident smell of the bathroom. She didn't like the idea that she'd gotten used to that smell.

After a few minutes of identifying a bunch of innocuous sounds outside the bathroom door and a couple of ominous rustling sounds that came from inside the bathroom, Maddy heard footsteps coming toward her. She froze, partly like a child who thinks being still would render her invisible and partly in real, identifiable fear.

The footsteps stopped right outside the bathroom door. Maddy waited, breathing through her mouth, hoping that the raspy sawing of her panicked breaths wasn't audible to the man standing on the other side of the door.

Then she heard the sound of a key sliding into a padlock.

Chapter Thirteen

Back when he and Tristan were kids, Zach had known where Boudreau lived. Now he wasn't sure. He stood in the middle of the clearing with his eyes closed, trying to remember back all those years. The pier was behind him, the path to Tristan's house was to his left and the seafood warehouse was about a mile straight ahead. So the path to Boudreau's stilt shack had to be to his right. But he'd already examined the ground in that direction. There was no hint of a path in the grass and weeds and vines that covered the ground. He'd also examined the branches of the trees and shrubs, but he couldn't find even one broken twig or branches to tell him that people had passed that way recently.

The way Boudreau had appeared, practically out of thin air, he had to have come that way. But how did he move through the thick brush of the bayou without breaking branches?

A cool breeze blew in off the Gulf, causing

Zach to shiver. He had on the same short-sleeved pullover shirt he'd worn to the sheriff's office. The temperature had been warm today, in the eighties, but on the coast, as the sun went down, the air cooled, especially if the breeze was off the Gulf. He figured by dark it might be as cool as sixty degrees. Not cold by any means, but he was sunburned after being outside without sunblock and he knew that he would feel chilly.

Dismissing those inane thoughts, he started in the direction he was sure Boudreau's cabin lay. That meant he'd be walking through brush and brambles and vines, but if he wanted to enlist Boudreau's help capturing the smugglers, which he did, then he had no choice. About three feet beyond the clearing, the heavy tangles of branches and vines thinned out and he finally could make out the path. It wasn't exactly as he remembered it, but it was heading in the right direction.

He pushed on until he finally came to a small clearing that was mostly hidden on all sides by swamp. Zach glanced around, looking for some sign that would tell him that this was Boudreau's place. But there was nothing except the stilt house itself.

Zach took one step toward the house and heard a shotgun being cocked. "Boudreau?" he called, holding his hands up. "It's me, Zach.

Tristan's friend. I just want to talk to you. Nothing else. I need your help with something."

He heard the second barrel of the shotgun cock. "Boudreau. Listen to me."

A shotgun blast hit just close enough to Zach's feet to knock dust up into his face, but not so close as to send a stray piece of shot toward him. He backed up a few steps and stood still, his hands still out and up. "I'm not moving, Boudreau. Sorry to disturb you. But I need this for Tristan's sake."

The large, thick wooden door swung open and Boudreau's face, dark and angry, appeared. He held his shotgun pointed right at Zach's midsection. Zach's belly contracted. "You a careless man, come here like this, you."

"I need your help, Boudreau, to stop the men who killed Tristan. Can I talk to you for just a minute?"

"There ain't no such thing as *just a minute,*" the old man yelled. "Besides, this is my place, and you had to walk through M'sieu Tristán's place to get here. You ain't got business either place, his nor mine."

"You're right," Zach said, his hands still raised. "I shouldn't have come. I'll work for you. I'll give you money for your time. Anything, if you'll just listen to me for—for five minutes."

There was a long pause as Boudreau studied Zach and muttered unintelligibly to himself.

Zach was worried about the man. The last time he'd talked to him he'd seemed happy enough to babble on about things Zach had no clue about. But he was seriously talking to himself now. Zach was sure that if he could hear him clearly, the words wouldn't make sense.

"Boudreau?"

"I can listen for free," Boudreau said. "You got five minutes."

"I know you told Maddy—the woman you talked to—that you thought the smugglers would come tonight. I think they will, too. When they do, I'd like to have your help to catch them and stop them from selling those guns. The Coast Guard will help us."

"Coas' Guard?" Boudreau said. "Why you done brought the Coas' Guard in to mess everything up?" He muttered to himself some more and shook his head. "I guarantee you," he said, his voice rising, "I don't want no Coas' Guard."

"I'm afraid you don't have a choice there," Zach said. "We can't do it by ourselves, Boudreau, and we need to do it tonight. It's the last new moon, you know. The night starts getting brighter after this."

"You ain't got to tell me that, you."

"Will you come down to the clearing with your shotgun and help me?"

Boudreau stepped back inside his shack. Zach waited. After at least three minutes, he began to get worried that Boudreau had dismissed him or forgotten about him. But finally the old Cajun emerged with his shotgun and wearing a stained vest that Zach could see was stuffed with extra shells.

Zach himself had his government-issue weapon, but he also had the automatic that Maddy had given him. He had a full magazine of bullets. But if he ran out of them, he wouldn't be able to reload. He'd have to switch to his own semiautomatic gun. "You ready to go?" Zach asked Boudreau.

"I reckon," the Cajun said. "I don't like this, me. Never took much truck with killing, animals nor men, but if that's what we have to do to stop those guns getting spread all over hell and creation, then that's fine, yeah."

When the two of them got to the clearing, it was beginning to get dark. "I don't know what time they'll get here, and I don't know how long we'll have to wait," Zach said. "But if we can, I want all the evidence I can get against them. So we should wait until they load the bags onto the wagon and push them all the way up to the warehouse. Then we'll nab them there. Hopefully, they'll think they're home free and that nothing can touch them.

"Home free," Boudreau said with a grin. "Olly olly oxen free."

Zach groaned inwardly. Boudreau had been comparatively rational so far, except for the muttering. But now he was sounding crazy again. "Boudreau, listen to me. Captain Reasoner will be here. He's going to tell us where he wants us to hide and what he wants us to do. Is that okay with you, Boudreau?" Zach asked. "He's a good guy and he knows what he's doing. We can count on him to help us catch these guys."

"Captain? He one of those oil rig captains?"

Zach shook his head. "Nope."

"That's good," Boudreau said before Zach had a chance to say anything else. "'Cause if it was that captain from that rig where M'sieu Tristán worked, I could of already caught him a while ago. When he come up here in one of them boats. He looked mean and mad."

"What? What are you talking about?"

"That captain on that rig. Couple hours or so. He let that boat go, just like it were nothing. It's probably tangled up in brush and weeds around one of them bends by now, where ain't nobody can see it. That ain't right, to let a boat go like that."

Zach's head was spinning. The captain of the

Pleiades Seagull was there at the dock? And he let his boat go? He had no idea if Boudreau knew what he was saying, but if even half of it was true…

Zach's stomach knotted. "Where did the captain go?"

"Me, I don't know. I didn't stick around to watch. All I know's he didn't come down my path today."

What Captain Reasoner told him about what he'd found on the *Pleiades Seagull* came back to him. He thought the captain might have abandoned ship using one of the lifeboats. But why? To Captain Poirier, the plan to smuggle the guns into the United States via Tristan DuChaud's old boat dock should be right on track. So what possible reason would he have to sneak ashore unannounced and alone, at that exact same spot. "I've got to get in touch with the captain," Zach muttered.

"What captain? Where? Not that one," Boudreau snapped in a panic. "I don't want him anywhere near—" he spat out a wad of tobacco "—anywhere near me," he finished sullenly, kicking up a rock with his toe like a scolded schoolkid.

"This is Captain Reasoner, remember? With the Coast Guard, Boudreau. He's a good guy."

"Coas' Guard. Me, I don't like the Coas'

Guard, neither. They ride up and down here and scare the fish and spill oil from those ugly boats."

"But then, you said it was okay if Reasoner helped us figure out where to hide until the men brought the guns ashore. Remember?" If he couldn't count on Boudreau, Zach was afraid their plan would fail. He needed the old man and his stealthy silence in the swamp to spot the boats and let the rest of the team know that they were docking. "We've got to stop the guns."

Boudreau shook his head. "You think I care about all them guns and such? You think that's what's bothering me? Naw. That don't bother me none. I don't care who got what guns. Why I wanna care about that? Ain't none of them coming after me. I just care about keeping the water clean and making sure nobody hurts M'sieu Tristán's land. That's all."

Zach stared at the Cajun. "I don't believe that," he said. "You said before you don't like killing."

Boudreau looked down at the ground and kicked a pebble. "Maybe I don't. I shoot when I got to, but I don't when I don't. So, when they get to where they getting, then what? We just going to shoot 'em?"

"No. Not at all. The Coast Guard is going to be waiting outside the seafood warehouse to grab them and their contraband as soon as they start loading the guns."

"Yeah. That's good. I don't want to shoot nothing— animal or person, unless there's a damn good reason," Boudreau said, nodding.

MADDY WISHED SHE could back away from the door, but there was no room in the tiny bathroom. She listened to the rattling of the padlock, then the metallic rasp as a key was inserted into the lock and turned. If she'd been able to see, she'd have watched the knob on the door turn, but she couldn't see the knob well enough, so she waited, tense and frightened, as the door opened and Captain Poirier's face appeared in her dark-adapted vision.

"Let's go," he said.

She stepped forward, wobbling. "I can't," she said. "I'm shaky and sick. I can't balance with my wrists cuffed."

With a growl, the captain grabbed Maddy's arm and pulled her along with him. She tried to walk steadily, but she'd told him the truth. She did feel sick from the awful odors. Sick and shaky. Maybe from lack of water or the suffocating, fetid heat in that tiny room. Poirier paid no attention, though. He just dragged her over to where a nail barrel sat on the ground.

"Sit. There." He made her sit on the barrel, with her hands still cuffed behind her.

She stared up at a tractor-trailer rig that barely fit into the warehouse. "What are you going to do with an eighteen-wheeler?" she asked.

"Don't worry about what I'm going to do," he said. "Worry about what's going to happen to you—" he bent over and got in her face "—if you don't *shut up*! Do you want me to stick a rag in your mouth—or something else?" He held up the gun, then pushed the barrel of it against her lips. "Open up," he said, his lips curling in what Maddy thought looked like a devil's mask but what he must have thought was a smile.

She sat there, unmoving. She couldn't open her mouth. If she let him stick the barrel of the gun into her mouth, the dynamic of their relationship would change and she'd be defeated. He was struggling for dominance right now because so far she'd managed to push him just enough to irritate him without going too far. But if she let him do this, he would know that she wasn't strong. Not in the way that courageous people are. He would find out that she would do anything to stay alive.

So she pressed her lips together, wincing at the soreness in her jaw, and shook her head without speaking. She had to keep quiet, although it went against her nature. She'd always talked her way out of things, but she had never faced a life-and-death situation before.

"I said, open your mouth." He pushed the barrel, pressing her lips hard against her teeth. "Or this gun barrel will go somewhere else."

She pulled her head back, trying to ease the pressure on her already bruised mouth. She still didn't say anything, didn't open her mouth and didn't look him in the eye.

Neither one of them moved for what seemed like a long time to Maddy. Then finally, Poirier took the gun away from her mouth with a disgusted grunt. She held her breath, praying he wasn't going to make good on what he'd said he would do if she didn't open her mouth.

But when she finally dared to lift her gaze, he was looking at his watch and starting to pace. He still held the gun, and she saw on the side where the lever was that he hadn't switched it from single-shot to multiple-shot.

Maddy waited, willing herself not to speak. Her hands were numb and swollen. Her arms ached from being pulled backward. There were too many sore and aching places on her face and mouth to count, and when she moved a certain way, something in her midsection, where he had punched her, hurt a lot.

She tried to flex her fingers and move her hands, but they were barely responsive. She wasn't sure how long circulation had to be cut off in the hands before they were permanently damaged. She was pretty sure it wasn't very long, and she was also pretty sure that if that short deadline had not already passed, it would soon.

As she tried to distance herself from the pain in her face and stomach and hands, her thoughts turned to Zach. She hoped to high heaven that he had gone back to the house and seen her clothes and suitcases still there. He would know she wouldn't take off in his car without her things. He'd know there was something wrong.

Please, Zach. Find me.

She felt her eyes filling with tears again, and despite her efforts, a quiet moan escaped past her throat.

Poirier looked up at her. His expression at first was dark and angry, but when he saw her crying, he smiled. Maddy had never seen anything as diabolical as that smile. She cringed as he walked over to her and, using the barrel of the gun, wiped a single tear off her cheek.

She shuddered and he smiled again. And she now knew with dreaded certainty that he was going to kill her, and her death would not be easy.

Chapter Fourteen

Captain Reasoner handed Zach a wireless earpiece. "This will let us talk hands free," Reasoner said, indicating the one in his ear. "Much more reliable than cell service around here."

Zach examined it. "Doesn't have to go far to be better than a cell phone in this area," he said wryly. "It can't be very long range, though, can it?"

"It does pretty well. Farther with line of sight, but we can easily stay in communication for eight to ten miles in this terrain."

Zach positioned the small device in his ear and took a second one to Boudreau. It took less explanation than he expected for the elderly Cajun to figure it out. Then the three of them, plus three Coast Guard officers, went over the plan one more time in order to make sure everyone, including Boudreau, knew exactly what was going down.

"Monsieur Boudreau," Reasoner said, "I'd

like you to stay here at the dock. You'll be the
best man to know when the boats are coming.
You let my men know as soon as you hear or
see something. Then you back off and my men
will do what they've been told."

"I got my shotgun, me, Captain," Boudreau
said. "Ain't never shot nobody," he said, then spit
on the ground. "But I can take down a dozen
birds with one shot—in season, of course." He
scowled, then muttered, as if to himself, "Don't
like to shoot 'em, but a man's gotta eat."

Zach exchanged a look with Reasoner.

"I don't think you'll have to shoot, *monsieur*,"
Reasoner said. "We don't want to alert the smugglers before they're inside the warehouse with
the transport truck. It's better for evidence."
Then he turned to Zach and reiterated what he'd
told him earlier. "I'll stay in the dock area with
Boudreau. You'll be with my men outside the
warehouse. The sheriff will be there, too, with
a couple of deputies. The takedown and arrest
will be a multidepartmental cooperative effort,
including the Coast Guard, NSA and local law
enforcement. That way, the anti-American con-
tingent will see a united front for the US."

Zach nodded. Boudreau kept fiddling with the
earpiece in his ear, seeming preoccupied with,
or maybe fascinated by, it. But when Reasoner
stepped up to shake his hand, he straightened

and held out his right hand, which did not tremble, and nodded like a seasoned military man.

Everyone took their assigned places and prepared for the most difficult part of the entire operation. The waiting.

ZACH HAD NO IDEA how much time had passed, when a voice spoke in his ear, rousing him from a near-drowsing state.

"Boat approaching." It was Reasoner. "Everyone ready. Officer Carter will take over from here. No noise. Out."

Zach tensed and took a deep breath, working on his focus. He waited for the feeling he called his SWAT Mode, where his mind and body worked together to keep him alert and confident. He felt it coming over him. He was ready, his weapon felt good in his hand. But for the first time ever, there was something missing.

When he and Maddy had worked together, they had melded together and formed a perfect pair, perfectly in sync, almost able to read each other's minds. Zach's SWAT Mode didn't even compare.

"The wagon is moving toward the warehouse," Reasoner spoke again. "Men on the path, be ready. Do not. Repeat. Do not engage. Defense only. Let them pass. Wait for my orders. Out."

Zach felt his muscles straining with tension. He breathed slowly and steadily in a conscious effort to stay in his heightened state of readiness. He couldn't forget how different and more complete he'd felt when teamed with Maddy. They'd shared each other's energy and passion and felt the sheer thrill of moving in such tightly woven sync that they might as well have been one entity.

He glanced to his right at the one Coast Guard officer he could see. The man looked back at him. They nodded at the same time. Then Zach heard the creak of metal against metal. It was the wagon, and the wheels sounded burdened, as if they were straining under a very heavy weight. He pulled back farther into the shadows. Under a sky with no moon, it was easy to hide. He'd just gotten situated and regained his focus when he saw the wagon.

He needed to know how many men were with it. There were two men in front of the wagon, pulling it as if they were oxen. Another man was behind, pushing the heavy vehicle. A fourth man appeared to be the lookout. He also retrieved any weapons that dropped onto the ground through tears in the canvas or a broken zipper.

The wagon passed without incident. Zach didn't move. He listened to the squeaky wheels until they'd gone around the warehouse. He heard a banging on the metal freight door and a voice calling out. These guys weren't very subtle. They acted as though they'd done this before. Maybe their dry runs hadn't been so skeletal after all. Light flared as the freight door opened to let the wagon in. Zach could see nothing but the light and shadows from where he was.

He knew that Captain Reasoner was in position across the street from the warehouse and was filming what was going on. He just wished Reasoner would get his assessment of the inside of the warehouse done and give them their orders.

Then he heard the little click that meant that Reasoner had turned on the microphone. "Tractor-trailer rig. White BMW rental car, 300 series. It appears the only people inside the building are a man, presumably the captain, and a woman, probably Agent Tierney of Homeland Security. She appears to be tied up or handcuffed."

Zach froze. Maddy was in there? Poirier had her tied up? He had to get to her.

"Winter, acknowledge." Reasoner's voice penetrated his thoughts and he realized the man had been talking for several seconds.

"Sorry, sir. Repeat?" Zach's face burned.

"Move in. Stay low. They have automatic

weapons. Use deadly force only if unavoidable. Carter's in charge. Winter, acknowledge."

"Yes, sir," Zach responded.

"Out."

Zach made sure the small automatic handgun was ready and that the large magazine was full of bullets. Then he started moving toward the freight door, staying in the underbrush and following alongside the Coast Guard men.

As he rounded the corner of the warehouse and was able to see in the door, he spotted Maddy. She was sitting on a barrel with her hands behind her back. She looked miserable and dejected, but there was something else not right about her.

Zach looked closer. Her cheek and forehead were an angry red, and there was a blue shadow on her jaw. "You son of a bitch," he whispered under his breath. He'd like to kill Poirier or whoever had done that to her.

He looked closer, trying to see if she had any other contusions. Then he did a double take. What was she doing? She was rocking back and forth, just slightly. Had she been drugged or hit so many times that she was dazed? Before he had time to puzzle out what she was doing, Captain Poirier came into view.

Poirier was directing the men to get the

wagon all the way inside the warehouse and close the door.

"Get ready," Reasoner's voice came in Zach's ear. "Don't let the door lock you out. Carter, engage your helmet camera. On your signal."

Carter was the man next to Zach. Out of the corner of his eye, Zach saw Carter press his earpiece to turn on the microphone and his helmet to switch on the camera. Just as Carter opened his mouth to speak, loud, angry shouts split the silence.

For an instant, everything stopped. The men in the warehouse froze, as did Poirier. Zach didn't move. Nor did Carter. Everyone waited to see who had been shouting.

Then Zach saw him. It was Murray Cho, the fisherman who'd bought the warehouse. He was holding a rifle at his waist, like any decent cowboy, and he walked steadily toward the open freight door. Once he gained the doorway, he adjusted the position of the rifle so it was pointing at Poirier.

"You!" Cho shouted. "All of you. Put your hands up." He had a faint accent, which served to make his words sound more ominous. "Hands up! This is my warehouse. I buy it when I moved here. Want to make a living fishing and selling shrimp. Now you are making my warehouse into den of thieves. I want to shoot all of you and make you stop."

Zach waited, holding his breath, wondering whether Cho would actually shoot. He tried to estimate how many men Cho could kill before one of them shot him. He was pretty sure the number wouldn't be high—maybe the fisherman might get off two rounds.

Zach looked at Carter, who looked back at him. Carter was caught between the proverbial rock and hard place. If he called for his men to attack, Cho and Maddy could be killed. If he told them to wait, Cho would certainly be killed and Maddy might be shot accidentally.

Just as Carter took a deep breath to speak, another man stepped out of the darkness on the shadowed side of the building, holding a shotgun. Zach realized it was Boudreau.

"No," he whispered. He had little faith in Boudreau, but he didn't want the man to be killed because he was doing Zach a favor.

"You too nice, Mr. Cho," he said. "Captain Poirier, I never took much truck with killing. But this is for M'sieu Tristán." He fired two shotgun blasts straight at Poirier. Both hit the middle of his chest. He went down in a double explosion of blood.

There was an instant of total silence, then Carter spoke a single word. "Go." Carter and the other two Coast Guard officers started firing. Zach started shooting, also. The four men who had been loading guns into the eighteen-wheeler took cover and began firing back. At the same time, Boudreau and Cho somehow disappeared.

In between shots, Zach tried to find Maddy, but the spot where he'd thought her barrel had been was empty. His heart and belly contracted. Had she been shot? Or had she had sense enough to throw herself onto the ground and duck away behind the boxes that lined the back third of the warehouse?

Zach took another precious few seconds to see if he could spot Boudreau and Cho. During that unguarded instant, two bullets slammed into his right shoulder. He'd never been shot before, but he had no doubt that what had hit him were bullets.

He tried to raise his hand and fire back but it didn't work. He couldn't move it. All he could do was drop to the ground right where he stood to keep from being hit again.

People were yelling, and the sound and smoke of gunfire filled the air. Zach thought he heard somebody say his name, but he was too busy trying to pick up the gun with his left hand and figure out how to hold it. But that hand was too clumsy. Back to the right hand. His arm had thick, red blood dripping down it, all the way down to his fingertips.

Chapter Fifteen

Maddy's numb hands fell apart as she succeeded in her efforts to saw through the cuff using the broken metal wheel on the barrel she'd been sitting on. The first thing she did was dive down behind the car, hoping that no one would sneak up behind her and shoot her before she had a chance to find a weapon.

She was able to get the strips off her wrists, but her hands were useless. She wrung them, then tried to flex her fingers, but they wouldn't move. Not a single one. Rubbing her hands together felt like watching someone else. It was surprisingly confusing, because her brain kept insisting that those totally disconnected hands were hers.

Then, when the feeling finally started to return, a hot, burning pain engulfed them. It felt as though someone had stuck them in a fire that was tended by a swarm of angry bees.

Outside of her pain, people were still shooting at each other and Zach had been shot. She'd seen it all. The spray of blood that turned the air pink when the bullet hit his shoulder, or had it hit his chest? Maddy's first instinct was to get up and run to him, but she couldn't. Her hands didn't work. If she tried to reach him, she could be shot, too.

Her hands were still on fire, but it seemed as though the burning pain had lessened. The swelling was going down, too. She could flex her fingers about halfway. She wrung them and shook them some more, moaning quietly the whole time because of the pain.

Something tickled the side of her nose. She tried to scratch it, but of course her fingers wouldn't work right. The tickle was about to drive her insane. Finally, she used her wrist to rub at the itchy spot and it came away streaked with blood.

Blood? Maddy clumsily wiped a finger across her forehead and felt a tender place. She must have gotten a scratch that was now bleeding. What had happened? Then she remembered. Poirier was shot and killed. She'd been close enough to him to be spattered with some of his blood, and one of the birdshot from the shotgun must have struck her on the forehead.

Poirier had been holding a gun, a loaded gun. She needed that gun. It would be on the floor somewhere near him. Pulling herself across the concrete floor by her elbows, she sneaked around the back of the car until she could see Poirier's body. It was obvious that he was dead. There was a lot of blood everywhere, but mostly in the hole in his chest. His face looked even more like a death mask, with his mouth stretched back into a horrible grin.

And there was his gun, only about three feet in front of her. She took a deep breath and crawled out into the open to get it.

ZACH CROUCHED AND PEEKED out from behind the tree where he'd fallen when the bullets had hit his shoulder. He had to find Maddy and see if she was okay. That damned barrel had rolled to one side up against the car. If she was close to it, she took the chance of being shot by either side.

The gunfire had slowed and in Zach's ear, Carter was talking to Reasoner about the situation.

"The captain of the *Pleiades Seagull* is down. Two shotgun blasts to the chest. He has four men with him. Two of them are injured. The other two have retreated into the cab of the eighteen-wheeler, but they haven't cranked it. Apparently, don't have keys."

"Can you rush the cab?"

"Plan to, sir, just as soon as they're out of

ammunition. Right now, they're in the equivalent of an armored truck."

"Our men?"

"Winter is down. Two to the shoulder, I believe. My other two are okay. Still firing at the truck occasionally, to let the two men know we're here and to draw fire. As soon as I feel their ammunition is depleted, we'll move in."

"I'll have the ambulance standing by," Reasoner said. "And the sheriff's men. Out."

Zach looked at his right hand, which was streaked with blood that had dribbled down from his shoulder to his fingertips. He tried moving his fingers, tried wiping them on his jeans. For some reason, although the shoulder was hurting a lot more, his hand was working better. He picked up the gun. Tried holding it. Not half bad.

Using the tree to steady himself, he got up from his crouching position and stood there for a few seconds. Once he'd decided that he wasn't going to pass out, he crouched down and headed back the way they'd come around the warehouse. If he remembered correctly from when he was a kid, there was an old wooden door on the back side of the building that had rotted at the bottom. There had been about a third of the door missing when he was young. Old man Beltaine had put a dirty piece of cloth over that bottom part and probably had never thought about it again.

Zach made it around the side of the building and found the old door, which looked exactly as he remembered. But he was breathing hard and feeling completely drained. He kicked at the bottom with his toe. Thank goodness Beltaine hadn't replaced the door. He got onto his hands and knees, feeling as if half his blood had drained out of him, and crawled through the bottom of the door into the warehouse.

Aware of what Carter had said about the men in the cab of the eighteen-wheeler, Zach lay flat on the concrete inside the door. Luckily, there was a pile of boxes near the door that hid him from the two men in the truck's cab. He wound through the boxes and stayed in the shadows until he'd worked his way around the perimeter of the building and was just about even with the back of his car. Just as he ducked and ran from the last box to hide behind the car, she crawled around the back tires on her elbows and knees, balancing a gun in the crook of her elbow.

She jumped when she realized there was someone there. Then she looked at him and immediately tears glistened in her eyes. She set the gun down and reached for him. "Oh, my God, Zach," she whispered. "I saw you get hit. Is it your shoulder? You're covered in blood."

"I'm okay. My hand's giving me some trouble, but I think I can hold a gun. Maybe even shoot it," he said, giving her a smile, then leaning down to kiss her.

She kissed him back, but the kiss didn't last very long because it was interrupted by the sound of a very big diesel engine trying to crank.

"They're going to get away!" Maddy said.

"I think they're trying to hot-wire the engine. I'm not sure they can do it."

The engine fired again, but coughed and died.

Maddy smiled at Zach. "Are you thinking what I'm thinking?"

He looked at her in bewilderment for an instant, then smiled back at her. "I'll bet I am. Hang on a sec." He pressed the send button on the earpiece he wore. "Winter to Carter. Maddy and I are going to arrest the two men in the truck cab. Don't shoot us."

He heard Carter's voice saying no, so he removed the earpiece and stuck it in his pocket.

"He said go ahead," he told Maddy and leaned in to give her a peck on the cheek. "Partner."

Maddy gestured that she would take the driver's side of the truck cab and let Zach have the passenger side. That side was closer and, for Zach's sake, she was betting that the stronger, better man had taken the driver's seat.

Her hands were almost back to normal. They felt tender and every so often fire would sear through a finger or her wrist, but they were working well enough for her to hold and operate her weapon.

As she crept toward the door, staying so close to the fender and tires of the cab that she was sure the men couldn't see her, she took a long breath and reveled in the feeling of power and connection she felt, now that she was with Zach again.

From those first few minutes when they'd moved together to make sure Sandy's bedroom was clear of intruders, she'd felt an intense and intimate bond with him. As if each of them knew what the other was about to do.

She waited to open the door to the cab until she was sure Zach was in place. It didn't take him long. Once she felt that he was ready, she took hold of the cab door, shouted, "Federal officers!" and yanked it open.

In unison with her shout, Zach yelled, "Drop your weapons. Now! Hands up!" And he opened the passenger door of the cab.

The man sitting in the driver's seat dropped the cables he was trying to twist together and reached for his weapon, which was lying on the floor near his right foot.

"Don't move!" Maddy yelled.

He pushed at her with his left hand and groped for the gun with his right. Maddy didn't anticipate his shove and barely reacted in time to avoid being pushed off the edge of the driver's-side door. However, she regained her balance instantly and coldcocked him on the back of the head with her pistol. "I said don't move," she said to him as he collapsed, dazed, back into the driver's seat.

While she handled the driver, Zach wrestled with the man on the passenger side. When he'd flung the door open, the man had pointed his automatic handgun directly at Zach's head. Or where he'd figured Zach's head would be.

But Zach had anticipated that possibility, so when he swung the door open, he stayed behind it. The man started firing before the door was completely open.

Once the burst of fire stopped, Zach ducked under the door and aimed his weapon directly at the man's groin. "I wouldn't move if I were you. And you really ought to drop your weapons. All of them. Otherwise…" He paused as he prodded the man's thigh. "I might miss and take out your femoral artery. I understand bleeding to death is a scary way to go."

Chapter Sixteen

"Zach? Are you all right?" It was Maddy.

"I'm fine. I'm calling the others." He slapped his ear then remembered that the earpiece was in his pocket. So he just yelled.

"Carter!" he shouted. "We've got 'em. Want to come and take them off our hands?" Yelling made him light-headed, so he backed up until he hit the fender of the car and leaned against it.

As he saw Carter and the other two men emerge from the trees where they'd taken cover, he called out to Maddy, "Good job, Tierney." But his voice didn't sound good to himself. It sounded weak and kind of thready.

"Same to you, Winter. How's your arm?"

"Oh, it's…okay."

The last thing he remembered was Carter relieving him of his weapon while another Coast Guard man ordered Zach's prisoner out of the truck and up against it, arms out and legs apart, to be frisked.

ZACH WOKE UP in a hospital bed with tubes and wires and bandages everywhere. It took him a few moments to orient himself. Once he did, he took a look at all the stuff that was attached to him. He was trussed up like a Thanksgiving turkey. His right arm was bandaged from shoulder to below the elbow, which made it impossible for him to move any part of it except his fingers. His left hand had an IV cannula stuck in the back. Zach saw black-and-blue marks on the hand where the nurses had apparently tried to insert the IV and failed. He couldn't move either hand. He was totally helpless.

He looked toward the door. It was closed. Nobody would hear him if he yelled. For a few moments, he lay there, willing himself to fall back to sleep. Instead, the events that had put him here kept rolling around in his head.

Boudreau shooting Poirier in cold blood, as if that had been his mission all along.

The man in the truck who had gone ghoulishly pale when Zach told him where he was going to shoot him.

Maddy, her hands swollen and blue and her wrists bisected by raw scrapes from some sort of restraint, crawling around the car, holding one of the automatic guns.

He shook his head. He didn't think he'd ever get over being amazed by her. She was the bravest person he may have ever known, with the possible exception of Tristan. In the whole time he'd known her—three days?—she'd never backed down from any challenge.

Actually, he amended, she had backed down once. When he'd told her he wanted her gone.

That had surprised him. He'd thought, hell, he'd *expected* a knock-down, drag-out fight that would likely end with him agreeing to let her stay. But she'd given up way too easily.

He closed his eyes. He'd had only one thing on his mind when he'd told her to leave. Her safety. He'd had to give her the choice, and he'd had to make it as easy as possible for her. This was not her fight. It was his. Tristan was his friend.

She had no reason to stay once her assignment had been terminated. The only thing that would accomplish would be to put her in danger, and for what? To help him. He'd done it to keep her safe, and he'd understood that she might take it as a rejection.

And she had.

His thoughts weren't particularly consecutive, connected or even coherent, he realized. He kept drifting off to sleep, waking up and drifting again. At some point during his sleep-driven musings, he was aware of someone telling him that the doctor had finished operating on his shoulder and that the anesthesia, plus something to help with the pain, might make him sleep. He nodded slowly. That was why he felt so tired.

He jerked awake suddenly. What was that? Something was beeping. He peered around. To his right and a little behind his head was an IV pole with a blue box on it with a flashing red light. That was where the beeping was coming from.

Damn it, if he could just move. Where was the nurse and why had they made it impossible for him to do anything for himself? He must have fallen asleep again, because the next thing he knew, someone was hanging a new bag of fluid and talking to him.

"Don't worry about that, Mr. Winter. Your IV pole beeps at the nurse's station as well as here in the room."

"What?"

The nurse laughed. "Not fun to fall asleep while you're talking, is it? You'll feel more alert and you'll start remembering things better within the next few hours. You're still under the effects of the sedation."

"What about if I'm thirsty, or my hand starts bleeding?" he said irritably.

"I'll just move the buzzer right here by your hand," she said, putting a white controller beside him. "You can reach it fine there."

"Thanks," he said ungraciously.

"I'll check on you in a little while," she said, heading for the door.

"What about my water? I'm thirsty."

"I'll send it in as soon as I get back to the nurse's station," she said cheerily as she walked out and shut the door.

"Send it in," he mocked, trying to swallow against his dry throat. Within a few seconds, he drifted off to sleep again.

MADDY SAT BESIDE Zach's bed and picked at the bandages on her wrists as she watched him sleep. She wasn't sure if being here when he woke up was a good idea.

His mother was driving over from Houston and would be here within the hour. And Maddy had a first-class ticket on a flight from New Orleans to DC that was leaving at 11:05 a.m., so if she was going to get a chance to talk to Zach alone, it had to be now.

The bandage on his right shoulder looked massive. The nurse who'd agreed to let her sit with him while he slept had explained to her that he'd taken two bullets in the shoulder. One had passed through muscle without too much damage. It would heal naturally. But the other bullet had torn through his rotator cuff. He needed surgery to repair the large tear and he would need physical therapy to regain full use of his shoulder. The nurse had acted as if it was no big deal, but to Maddy, it sounded as if Zach was going to have a difficult and painful recovery ahead of him.

She looked at the time on her phone. His mother would be here in about forty minutes. Her time was running out. She didn't want to wake him. According to the nurses, he'd been sleeping a lot and he was pretty grouchy when he was awake. But she'd been called to DC for debriefing and reassignment and she had no idea where she might end up. She needed to talk to him before she left and possibly never saw him again.

A quiet gasping sob escaped her lips. Her hand shot to her mouth immediately, too late, of course, to stop the sob, but possibly in time to keep any others from escaping.

Zach stirred and mumbled something.

Maddy froze, staring at him, confusion tearing at her insides. Should she wake him or not? She wanted to see him, but what if he didn't want to see her? What would she say then? *Sorry, wrong room, sorry, wrong guy, sorry, wrong life?*

She shook her head and rubbed her temple. This was probably a big mistake. And now his mother would be here in thirty-five minutes.

"Maddy?"

She jumped. "Zach?" she said in a strangled voice. "I didn't mean to wake you." He turned his head on the flat hospital pillow, trying to see her around the bed rails and the IV pole.

"Come here," he whispered.

With her heart throbbing in her throat, she stood and walked around the bed. "Hey," she said, trying to smile. The trouble was that when she saw his intense green eyes looking so weak and tired, she wanted to cry. "How're you feeling?"

"I'm thirsty as hell," he croaked. "Can't even talk."

"I'll get you some water," she said, turning toward the door.

"Don't leave."

She stopped. "O-okay." She came back to the side of the bed. "Do you want me to call someone to bring it?"

"Maybe later."

"Are you hurting?"

He shook his head, then craned his neck, trying to look behind him. "Do you see that stupid controller back there? It's white, with a cord that's thick as a rattlesnake."

Maddy saw a white cord and followed it. "Here. It fell off the side of the bed. Do you want me to call for water now?"

He looked up at her. "No. What are you doing here?"

"I was— I just—"

"Damn it, Maddy." He tried to reach for her hand with his left hand, the one with the IV in it. "Let me see your hand."

"What? Why?" She didn't move. She didn't know what he wanted, but then that had been the problem all along, hadn't it? She'd known she wanted him from the first time she'd laid eyes on him, but she'd never been able to figure him out. As in sync as they were, she always knew he was holding something back. One part of himself that she'd never been able to penetrate.

"Let me see your hand," he repeated.

She held her right hand close to his left. He took it and turned it over, looking at the palm, then turned it to examine the back. Letting it go, he looked up at her again. "What about you?" he asked, running his tongue across his dry lips.

"I'm fine," she said. "I'm good."

"No," he said, shaking his head. "No, you're not. There's something wrong. What is it? Is it something about the case?"

She didn't answer.

"Something about Boudreau? Or Tristan?"

She shook her head. "No. Nothing like that. Boudreau is out on bail. One of the sheriff's deputies arrested him for shooting Poirier, but it sounds like he'll get off with simple manslaughter and time served."

"Then it's you." He rested his head back on his pillow and licked his lips again. "What is it, Maddy? You want to tell me something. Go ahead. Spit it out. I can take it. Is it about Poirier? What did he do to you? I know he hurt you."

"I'm fine, Zach," she said, then took a long breath. "He hit me in the face and once in the stomach. But that was nothing. I'm tough."

Zach nodded. "Yeah."

Maddy had never felt so out of her element. She would never forgive herself if she got this far and didn't say what she needed to say, although right that instant she felt as if she'd rather be shot and punched in the stomach than to tell him. No. She had to tell him. She might end up living out the rest of her life never knowing what might have been. And she didn't like not knowing. Anything, no matter how bad, was better than the unknown.

"Zach, I got your message on my phone."

He frowned, then opened one eye. "My message?" he repeated as a question.

She nodded and lifted her chin. "You said, 'I'd like to have you with me, if you want to be.'"

"Did I?"

"Zach, can you look at me, please?"

He opened his eyes and scowled at her. "What?"

"Did you mean it?"

"Mean what?"

Maddy felt the tears swelling up in her throat, getting ready to pour from her eyes. "You know what. Do you have to be like this?"

He closed his eyes again. "I'm tired, Maddy. What is it you want?"

She sighed, it was a halting, hiccuping sound. "I just wanted to tell you something before I leave to go back to DC."

He lay there for a long time with his eyes closed. Then about the time Maddy had decided he'd fallen asleep, he opened his eyes and looked at her. He wasn't scowling or glaring or frowning or even looking at her blandly. His green eyes had turned dark and his mouth had thinned. "DC? You're leaving me, Madeleine Tierney?"

She blinked and the first of what she knew were going to be a lot of tears slid down her cheeks. She tried to smile. "I'm afraid I have to. I'm being called to DC for debriefing and reassignment."

He nodded and looked down at the IV in his arm. "I understand," he said. "Was that it?"

She swiped tears from her cheeks with the back of her hand. "Sorry?"

"Was that what you wanted to tell me?"

"No," she said, shaking her head. "No." She laughed shortly. "No. I just wanted to tell you— I wanted to say…" she said, her voice fading.

Could she tell him what she really needed to say? Was she even capable of opening enough to him to tell him that she'd never felt the way she did when he looked at her with that faintly bewildered expression that told her he wanted her and he wasn't sure why? Could she tell him all of that, or any of it?

After a few moments of utter silence in the room, Maddy took a deep breath. "I love you, Zach Winter. I don't need you to say anything or do anything or…anything. I just needed to say it." She swiped at her tears one more time. Then she adjusted her cross-body purse and turned to leave.

"Maddy?"

She looked back at him. "Yes?" she said cheerily.

"Come here."

"I really ought to be going. I've got a plane to catch in New Orleans tomorrow."

"Please?"

The tone of his voice was odd. Maddy turned to look at him and saw the glimmer of tears in his eyes. "Zach? Are you okay? Is something hurting? Should I call a nurse?"

"Yes. Yes. No." He smiled. "There's only one

cure for what's hurting me. You have to stay here. Otherwise my heart's going to shatter."

Maddy blinked. "What? Your…heart?"

"Give me your hand."

Maddy didn't hesitate this time. She held out her hand to him. He took it and pulled on it gently.

"Kiss me, Maddy," he said, and she did.

The door to the room swung open and a woman walked in.

Maddy jumped backward as if she'd been pushed. She sent Zach a look, then turned to face the woman, who looked to be in her early fifties. She was not as tall as Maddy, but she had a regal bearing, and her clothes and makeup were impeccable. She was holding a glass of water and there was something in her green eyes that told Maddy immediately who she was.

His mother, Maddy thought. And she'd seen them kissing. This could get awkward.

"Mom?" Zach said. "What are you doing here?"

"Zach, my goodness, look at you. You look like a mummy with all those bandages. Please tell me that you're all right. Otherwise I'm going to start crying and my makeup will get all streaky."

Zach laughed, then moaned. "Oh. Don't make

me laugh, Mom. Hey, is that water?" Zach demanded. "Give it here. I'm dying of thirst."

His mother put the water in his hand and he turned it up and drank half of it. "Ah," he said. "Thank you." He turned the glass up again.

"Zach?" his mother said. "Who is this?" She turned to Maddy. "Hello. Are you a social worker or…?"

"Mom!" Zach snapped, then winced in pain. "What have I told you about grilling my friends?"

"What?" she said. "What did I say?"

Maddy opened her mouth to answer, but Zach's mother had turned away.

Zach talked around gulps of water. "This is Maddy, Mom. She's not a social worker. She works for Homeland Security. I'm going to marry her."

He finished the last of his water while Maddy and his mother stared at him, speechless.

Epilogue

Two months later, Sandy was in her kitchen in Bonne Chance, when the phone rang. It was Maddy Tierney. "Maddy, hi. I was just thinking about you. How are you? How's Zach?"

"I'm fine and Zach's doing really well. He's almost a hundred percent. But I called to find out how you are. I called Mrs. DuChaud's number, but she said you were back in Bonne Chance."

Sandy cradled her belly in one hand while she held the phone with the other. "I just got here yesterday. I couldn't stay away any longer. This is my home. It was our home, Tristan's and mine, and it will be mine and the baby's."

"Speaking of the baby. What's the latest? Did that little thing ever fall off?"

Sandy laughed. "No. He's definitely a boy, a big boy, according to the doctor. Oh, Maddy, I wish—"

Maddy was silent for a beat, then she said, "I know, honey."

Of course Maddy knew what she was thinking. It was heartbreaking that Tristan would never see his son, and even more so that his child would never know him. "You didn't call to hear me whine. Tell me what's going on with you. I suppose you've heard all the news from here."

"I'm not sure if I've heard everything," Maddy said, as good at evading questions as she'd ever been.

Sandy poured herself a glass of purple juice and sat down at the kitchen table. "First of all, Boudreau didn't go to trial, but he didn't go to jail, either. I'm not sure what happened there, but he's back at his cabin. Mr. Cho and his son moved to Gulfport to try their hand at netting shrimp. Mr. Cho decided there was something wrong with Bonne Chance if smugglers could shoot up his warehouse. Oh, but listen to this. He came by to see me before he left. He wanted to apologize for his son peeking in my window and making me scream," Sandy said. "I told you I didn't dream that."

"Oh, Sandy, I believed you. I promise I did."

"I know, I know. So is there any more information from your end? Has anyone officially said that my husband's death wasn't an accident?"

Maddy didn't speak for a beat. "They're looking into it. I'm not in the loop, but Zach told me that the men who were taken into custody are being offered deals if they'll talk about who their boss was working for. So far, none of them have taken the offer. Also, they're investigating the company that owned the oil rig."

"So your answer is no. There's nothing official that says Tris's death was anything but an accident."

"That's true," Maddy said with a sigh. "But don't give up."

"Don't worry," Sandy responded. "Oh! I do have some good news. Speaking of the company that owned the oil rig. They set up a trust fund for the baby."

"Lee Drilling? Wow. Vernon Lee is one of the wealthiest men in the world. He probably did it for the publicity, so I hope the trust fund is huge."

"Huge doesn't begin to describe it. I'm having to get lawyers to help me figure out what to do with it. The company sent a lovely letter saying how much they mourned Tristan's death and—" She stopped and cleared her throat. "You know. All the usual stuff."

"I'm so glad. That will be a relief for you. Now you won't have to worry about you and the baby, and you won't have to go through all the pain and heartache of suing them."

"Yeah," Sandy said absently, looking outside. The sun had gone down and the sky was darkening. It was the gloaming of the day. The one time when Sandy could become maudlin if she wasn't careful. She sat back in the kitchen chair and patted her tummy where she knew the baby's little behind and legs were. "You're going to make me ask, aren't you?" she said.

"Make you ask what?" Maddy said innocently.

"Don't give me that innocent tone. I can hear you laughing. I'm not proud. Please tell me what's going on with you and Zach."

Maddy started talking about her plans to move from New Orleans to Fort Meade, Maryland, where Zach was, and that a few weeks ago he'd visited her and given her an engagement ring.

Sandy squealed. "That's so wonderful! Congratulations. You two were meant for each other. When's the wedding?" The baby kicked her. He was restless, so Sandy stood up and walked over to the French doors and looked out.

Yesterday, she'd walked over to the dock just before sundown. About the time the sun disappeared below the horizon, she'd spotted something diving and swimming in the water. It was hardly more than a silhouette in the waning light, but before she could tell whether it was a fish, a dolphin or maybe even a person, it had disappeared.

"Sandy?"

"Hmm? What? Oh," Sandy said. "I'm sorry. I guess I was thinking about the baby."

"Anyway, as I was saying, we want you and the baby up here for the wedding."

"Of course!" Sandy replied. "I wouldn't miss it for the world. When and where is it?"

"Sandy, are you okay? I just spent, like, five minutes talking about when and where. Are you okay?"

"Sure. Just daydreaming, I suppose. I'm sorry."

"Please. You're pregnant. You get a pass. Okay, I've got to go. The pizza guy is ringing the doorbell. Zach will be calling in a minute. He and I are having pizza together in different cities."

Sandy smiled. "Tell him I said hi. You two take care of each other, okay?"

Maddy said they would and hung up.

The day was waning into night. The sun had set. It was gloaming. It was too late to walk to the dock, or to see anything in the water if she did. With a sad smile, Sandy cradled her tummy and watched the last of the light fade into darkness.

* * * * *

Mallory Kane's BAYOU BONNE CHANCE
continues next month with
SECURITY BREACH.
Look for it wherever Harlequin Intrigue books
and ebooks are sold!

LARGER-PRINT BOOKS!

HARLEQUIN

Presents®

GET 2 FREE LARGER-PRINT NOVELS PLUS 2 FREE GIFTS!

YES! Please send me 2 FREE LARGER-PRINT Harlequin Presents® novels and my 2 FREE gifts (gifts are worth about $10). After receiving them, if I don't wish to receive any more books, I can return the shipping statement marked "cancel." If I don't cancel, I will receive 6 brand-new novels every month and be billed just $5.30 per book in the U.S. or $5.74 per book in Canada. That's a saving of at least 12% off the cover price! It's quite a bargain! Shipping and handling is just 50¢ per book in the U.S. and 75¢ per book in Canada.* I understand that accepting the 2 free books and gifts places me under no obligation to buy anything. I can always return a shipment and cancel at any time. Even if I never buy another book, the two free books and gifts are mine to keep forever.

176/376 HDN GHVY

Name	(PLEASE PRINT)	
Address		Apt. #
City	State/Prov.	Zip/Postal Code

Signature (if under 18, a parent or guardian must sign)

Mail to the **Reader Service:**
IN U.S.A.: P.O. Box 1867, Buffalo, NY 14240-1867
IN CANADA: P.O. Box 609, Fort Erie, Ontario L2A 5X3

**Are you a subscriber to Harlequin Presents® books
and want to receive the larger-print edition?
Call 1-800-873-8635 today or visit us at www.ReaderService.com.**

* Terms and prices subject to change without notice. Prices do not include applicable taxes. Sales tax applicable in N.Y. Canadian residents will be charged applicable taxes. Offer not valid in Quebec. This offer is limited to one order per household. Not valid for current subscribers to Harlequin Presents Larger-Print books. All orders subject to credit approval. Credit or debit balances in a customer's account(s) may be offset by any other outstanding balance owed by or to the customer. Please allow 4 to 6 weeks for delivery. Offer available while quantities last.

Your Privacy—The Reader Service is committed to protecting your privacy. Our Privacy Policy is available online at www.ReaderService.com or upon request from the Reader Service.

We make a portion of our mailing list available to reputable third parties that offer products we believe may interest you. If you prefer that we not exchange your name with third parties, or if you wish to clarify or modify your communication preferences, please visit us at www.ReaderService.com/consumerschoice or write to us at Reader Service Preference Service, P.O. Box 9062, Buffalo, NY 14240-9062. Include your complete name and address.

HPLP15

LARGER-PRINT BOOKS!

GET 2 FREE LARGER-PRINT NOVELS PLUS
2 FREE GIFTS!

HARLEQUIN®

Romance

From the Heart, For the Heart

YES! Please send me 2 FREE LARGER-PRINT Harlequin® Romance novels and my 2 FREE gifts (gifts are worth about $10). After receiving them, if I don't wish to receive any more books, I can return the shipping statement marked "cancel." If I don't cancel, I will receive 4 brand-new novels every month and be billed just $5.09 per book in the U.S. or $5.49 per book in Canada. That's a savings of at least 15% off the cover price! It's quite a bargain! Shipping and handling is just 50¢ per book in the U.S. and 75¢ per book in Canada.* I understand that accepting the 2 free books and gifts places me under no obligation to buy anything. I can always return a shipment and cancel at any time. Even if I never buy another book, the two free books and gifts are mine to keep forever.

119/319 HDN GHWC

Name   (PLEASE PRINT)

Address   Apt. #

City   State/Prov.   Zip/Postal Code

Signature (if under 18, a parent or guardian must sign)

Mail to the **Reader Service:**
IN U.S.A.: P.O. Box 1867, Buffalo, NY 14240-1867
IN CANADA: P.O. Box 609, Fort Erie, Ontario L2A 5X3
Want to try two free books from another line?
Call 1-800-873-8635 or visit www.ReaderService.com.

* Terms and prices subject to change without notice. Prices do not include applicable taxes. Sales tax applicable in N.Y. Canadian residents will be charged applicable taxes. Offer not valid in Quebec. This offer is limited to one order per household. Not valid for current subscribers to Harlequin Romance Larger-Print books. All orders subject to credit approval. Credit or debit balances in a customer's account(s) may be offset by any other outstanding balance owed by or to the customer. Please allow 4 to 6 weeks for delivery. Offer available while quantities last.

Your Privacy—The Reader Service is committed to protecting your privacy. Our Privacy Policy is available online at www.ReaderService.com or upon request from the Reader Service.

We make a portion of our mailing list available to reputable third parties that offer products we believe may interest you. If you prefer that we not exchange your name with third parties, or if you wish to clarify or modify your communication preferences, please visit us at www.ReaderService.com/consumerschoice or write to us at Reader Service Preference Service, P.O. Box 9062, Buffalo, NY 14240-9062. Include your complete name and address.

HRLP15